Whalesinger

Other books by
Welwyn Wilton Katz

Witchery Hill
False Face
The Third Magic
(Margaret K. McElderry Books)

WELWYN
WILTON KATZ
·
Whalesinger

Margaret K. McElderry Books
New York

Margaret K. McElderry Books
Macmillan Publishing Company
866 Third Avenue
New York, NY 10022

Published simultaneously in Canada by
Douglas & McIntyre/Groundwood Books Ltd.

Printed and bound in Canada

10 9 8 7 6 5 4 3 2 1

Library of Congress Cataloging-in-Publication Data
Katz, Welwyn Wilton.
    Whalesinger / Welwyn Wilton Katz—1st ed.
      p.   cm.
    Summary: A scientific field trip on the California
coast near the possible site of a sunken treasure ship
from Francis Drake's expedition brings together two
teenagers, an emotionally isolated boy and a girl who
is discovering she shares an empathic bond with two
gray whales in the area.
    [1. Whales—Fiction. 2. California—Fiction.
3. Buried treasure—Fiction.] I. Title.
      PZ7.K15746Wh 1990 [Fic]—dc20
          90-34091 CIP AC
          ISBN 0-689-50511-6

This book is dedicated to Albert and Meredith, who experienced the magic of Point Reyes and loved it with me; and to Catharine and Barbara and Syd and Lynda, who stood by me during the writing of *Whalesinger*, and afterward; and to Doug, who taught me about perfect meeting places and gave me one of my own.

ACKNOWLEDGMENTS

I want to thank Ravenna Helson of Berkeley, California, who lent me her cottage in Point Reyes on one of my visits and was helpful in many other ways; Robert Marx, of Indiatlantic, Florida, whose books on diving and salvaging treasure were very useful and from whose long telephone conversation I learned what it is really like to scuba dive in Drake's Bay; John L. Sansing, Superintendent, Point Reyes National Seashore, who kindly answered my many questions about the legal implications of salvaging treasure in Point Reyes; Tom Forster, a ranger at Point Reyes, who got me a lot of information about the summer appearances of mother and baby gray whales at Drake's Bay; William D. Maxwell, Senior Marine Biologist, State of California Department of Fish and Game, who sent me a lot of information about gray whales and answered a great many long and detailed questions; Mike Clough, Canada Customs, who was very helpful dealing with customs laws on treasure; and my friends, Jean Little and Claire MacKay, whose early enthusiasm for this novel provided more than just encouragement. I also gratefully acknowledge the financial support of the Canada Council, without which the writing of this book would have been infinitely more difficult. Finally, I would like to mention Warren L. Hanna, whose book *Lost Harbor* (University of California Press, Berkeley, 1979), a carefully documented and reasoned discussion of Sir Francis Drake's probable landfall on the California coast, was of immense help in my own research.

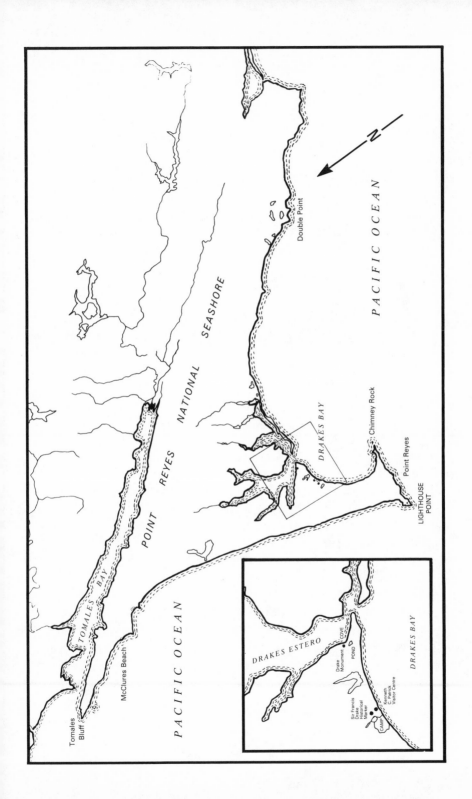

CHAPTER ONE

"GREAT PLACE, ISN'T IT?" JONAS ANDER-son said.

He was a ruddy-faced, sturdy man with piercing gray eyes. In the short time Nick had known him, he'd learned that it didn't always matter whether he answered Dr. Anderson's questions or not. Shoulders hunched, Nick stared out at Drake's Bay and said nothing.

They had climbed a zigzag path up the bluffs behind the Visitors' Center, ignoring the barbed-wire fence at the top to stand at the very edge of the cliff. The drop was sheer and raw, its crumbling, chalky face falling unbroken to the sand-and-pebble beach far below. There was no vegetation on the cliffside, and none on the beach. The erosion was too continual. Nick wanted to step back onto the thick pad of dry grass covering the uplands behind him, but he shoved his hands into his jacket pockets and stayed where he was.

On the map of California, Point Reyes had looked like a jackal's head, with the curving shoreline of Drake's Bay for the throat. Now, standing high on the edge of that shoreline, Nick tried to make out the jackal. To the south-west, the sharp point of Chimney Rock could be imagined as making a bottom edge for the jackal's muzzle; more than twice as far away to the southeast, Double Point marked the beginning of the neck. The long, pointy ears that were Tomales Point, away to the north on the ocean side of the peninsula, were entirely invisible, as was the upper edge of the muzzle at perilous Lighthouse Point, only a few miles west of Chimney Rock but hidden by hills.

It was colors, not shapes, that jumped out at Nick now that he was here. Against the parched silvery taupe of the grassy uplands the vivid sky was matched, three hundred feet down, by the glittering blue bay, curling white-tipped against the shore. Blue water, blue sky, a white ship anchored picturesquely in the middle, stark white cliffs swooping to the right and left. Winter colors, for all that it was summer. Nick hunched deeper into his jacket.

"You can see why I wanted to bring you up here," Dr. Anderson went on. He made a sweeping gesture to the right, taking in the Visitors' Center below them, the parking lot, the tarmac trail leading up out of it to the camp on the bluff opposite them. "The campsite's almost as high, of course, but all the tents and people over there spoil the feeling of the place. Not that I'm complaining. I'd never have thought we'd be able to get permission to camp at all. When I made my first erosion study here I had to get a room way out in Olema."

He paused, staring as if mesmerized over the bay. "Are those the Farallons, out there? By God, they are! See, Nick?—those lumpy little islands on the horizon? Twenty-eight miles away, if you can believe it."

Nick looked. Islands? Those little bumps? They hardly counted. Everywhere else was water, an eternity of untruncated sea. It was totally unlike Vancouver. Here there were no buildings to interrupt the view, no trees leaning out, no Vancouver Island, bigger than Belgium, sitting on a misty horizon and claiming it for its own. Here there was only one edge, and that was right in front of him, razor sharp with erosion, the voracious water licking at it.

"I've never seen them this clear in summer. I told you,

didn't I, Nick, that Point Reyes has the foggiest summers on the whole west coast?"

"Yes," Nick said, "yes, you did."

Dr. Anderson had told Nick considerably more than that about Point Reyes. Sitting with his feet up on his desk in his jumbled office at the University of British Columbia, he'd talked about the wildlife in Point Reyes and the rangers and the dairy farms and the visitors' centers. He'd gotten out a map and traced out half a dozen of the point's hiking trails, one of which went right alongside the San Andreas Fault to the epicenter of the earthquake that had almost destroyed San Francisco in 1906. That had happened, he said, because the two sides of the fault were moving in different directions. Most of Point Reyes was jerking its way north at the rate of about two inches a year, causing it to rub against the rest of California, which wasn't.

"Builds up strain," Dr. Anderson had explained. "Sooner or later the bedrock can't take it anymore. There'll be another big earthquake there in the next decade or two. Won't bother Point Reyes much, though. It's mostly tall buildings that cause the trouble in earthquakes, and Point Reyes hasn't got any. But San Francisco had better watch out!"

Nick had forced himself to listen carefully to the lecture on plate tectonics that followed. It was a strange way to conduct a job interview, but maybe Dr. Anderson was going to ask him to spout it all back later. An intelligence test, of sorts. And Nick needed this job. For someone seventeen years of age and just out of high school, summer jobs weren't all that easy to get. A job that would allow him to work with a computer, that paid twelve hundred a month, and best of all, that would be located far away from Vancouver, was not something he dared to risk.

After plate tectonics, Dr. Anderson had switched to history. "Did you know Francis Drake is thought to have careened the *Golden Hind* in Point Reyes? It was just before he attempted his first Pacific crossing. What a sailor! Insane, of course. Had to be. Sailing out onto that vast ocean, no charts, and for all he knew, scurvy, starvation, shipwreck, and cannibals ahead of him. Or what happened to Magellan." Dr. Anderson made a cheerful, throat-slitting gesture. "But Drake was luckier, or smarter; anyway, the Pacific let him alone long enough to cross it. First white man ever to come to Point Reyes, was our Drake. He called it Nova Albion—New England, get it? All because of the white cliffs."

He hummed a few bars of "The White Cliffs of Dover," then swooped into another subject, the history behind the marine sanctuary now centered on Point Reyes. Finally the interview had wound down. There was no test. There wasn't even a formal offer of employment. All Dr. Anderson did was stand up and shake Nick's hand.

"Pack for roughing it," he warned cheerfully. "You can fly down the last week of June. I'll be there a week or two before you, but I'll pick you up at San Francisco airport. Public transportation in rural California is awful."

As an afterthought, on his way out the door, Dr. Anderson had lent Nick a book about Point Reyes and its history. Nick had shoved it into his suitcase before leaving for the airport this morning, but he hadn't read it. Dr. Anderson had said enough about Point Reyes to last anybody a lifetime.

It was what Dr. Anderson hadn't said that bothered Nick. Nothing about camping out for an entire summer. Nothing about the fact that instead of a decent workspace with a solid roof overhead and a computer with a hard disk drive, Nick was going to have to manage with an outdated laptop computer on a rickety card table in a tent.

When he was younger Nick had loved camping. But he hadn't camped for two years, not since the last time he'd gone with Richard, just the two of them canoeing through the wilderness. Almost a month of setting up camp when dusk fell; fishing for their suppers; sitting up late over the campfire; the usual Boy Scout stuff. His brother had often gone wilderness camping, even on his own, even in the winter when the bad weather would have stopped anybody else. You could talk about thin ice and bogs and wolves until you were blue in the face, and Richard would just smile, and pack his kit, and go. He swam through danger the way other people swam through backyard pools, too big, too powerful to notice that he was out of his element.

Point Reyes, Nick reminded himself; living and working in a tent scarcely big enough to hold the card table. He could manage the living part. But analyzing massive amounts of data on a laptop computer with such limited storage? To say nothing of the lousy monitor! And running on batteries, and only four packs provided, and no electricity in the camp to recharge them! And worst of all, no sign of a printer. How could anybody have a computer without a printer?

Dr. Anderson had turned his back on the wind blowing off the sea and was stuffing tobacco in his pipe. "You'll be wanting to get your things unpacked, I guess, and maybe meet a few people. After that I could drive you to Lighthouse Point. You really shouldn't miss that view on a day like today. In spring the tourists line up there for miles to see the gray whales migrating northward from their calving places in southern California. Pity we're too late for that. The whales'll all be up in the Arctic by now."

"Dr. Anderson," Nick said. He cleared his throat nervously.

"Mmm?" Dr. Anderson was trying to get his pipe going.

"I don't know how I'm going to manage without a printer." It came out in a rush.

"I thought I'd told you. You'll be using the one on the ship."

13

"The ship?"

"Out there." Dr. Anderson pointed to the anchored ship. She was too big and white to be an ordinary fishing boat, though she had the look of one. Nick tried to read the name on her bow, but she was too distant.

"Does she belong to you? What's she called?"

Dr. Anderson frowned. "Wait a minute. Your dad didn't tell you?"

"Why would he?"

"When he asked me to give you this job, he promised he would tell you the ship was part of the deal."

"*Dad* asked you to hire me? But I thought—he said he'd heard you needed someone, but I didn't think—"

"You do know what this summer's all about, don't you, Nick?"

"It's a field trip," Nick said defensively. "You're doing some kind of erosion study."

"And who do you think is paying?"

"My father's grant pays for *his* research. I thought—"

"You thought I had a grant," Dr. Anderson said, cold and almost angry sounding. For a minute his lips clamped tight. "And what about the other scientists in the camp? Twelve people; more, counting the research assistants. Who's paying for them? Who flew them down here, half of them all the way from Canada? Who organized the camp? Who hired the cook?"

"How do I know? Somebody got a big grant. You all did. How do I know?"

"The grant that could fund this summer doesn't exist! We've been hired, boy; we're here to do a job. We'll do it the best way we can, and we won't let the foundation tell us what data to find and what to ignore, but the fact remains, in money matters we do what we're told. So if the foundation decides that we should use the ship out there to recharge our batteries and do our lab work and

14

develop our photographs and even for God's sake take a shower, then that's what we have to do, see?"

The foundation. Nick felt sick. He looked again at that white ship out in the bay. It didn't look as if it had ever been anything but white. But maybe you could get rid of smoke stains. Maybe you could varnish over the places where blood had spattered like a dropped can of red paint. Collect up the pieces. Clean up the mess.

His voice came out small and hard, like something too tightly wrapped. "Foundation?" His face was pinched with the effort needed to contain his thoughts. "It's the Conservocean Foundation, isn't it? It's Dr. Ray bloody Pembroke and his Save the stinking Ocean Fund. And that ship"—his voice went higher—"that ship's the *Leviathan*. Isn't it? Isn't it?"

"I'm sorry," Dr. Anderson said helplessly.

"You're sorry. My brother died working for that man on that ship, and you're sorry."

"Listen, Nick. I know about Richard. If I'd thought for one minute that you held his death against Pembroke—"

Nick's eyes were blazing. "If Pembroke hadn't—"

"Wait a minute, let me finish. If I'd known how you felt, I wouldn't have given you this job. Your father may have seen the job as some kind of psychotherapy for you, but what he *said* was that you needed the money and could do with a summer away from home. He also said that you were great on a computer, a solid *A* student, and a hard worker. That was all. He said he'd tell you about the Pembroke connection, and that he didn't think it would be a problem for you. I believed him, because it wasn't a problem for *him*, see? And Nick, I needed somebody exactly like the kid he described. I needed a bright kid who could manage any kind of computer problem, who was agile enough to go after data on steep cliffs, and who wouldn't mind being isolated from other young

15

people for the summer. I still need that person, Nick. So what are we going to do about it?"

Slowly Nick pulled his hands out of his pockets. "I could kill my father," he said, coldly and clearly. Then he swiveled on his heel and walked away.

The waters of the calving place were warm and languid, heady with growth and decay. Two whales alone remained of all that had gathered here, a mother and her calf. The rest had gone long before, the males first, then the mated females, and last, the mothers and their calves. This mother had given birth late, and it had been difficult. She had stayed in the calving place longer than she should, waiting for her calf to grow stronger. It was still very young, barely half weaned, but the mother knew it was time to leave. She had dived to the bottom of the lagoon over and over again, filtering the bottom mud through the fringed curtain of silky baleen in her mouth, but there was not nearly enough food there to satisfy her vast body. There would be less as the sun burned hotter.

The mother thought of her People, already gathering at the summer meeting place in the north. There, in bays shimmering silver under a glacial sun, they would be feeding, sucking hard-backed creatures from the icy silt, straining them between tongue and baleen and swallowing unhurriedly under a sky that never went dark and a wind that blew of silence.

Time, my calfling, she sang, *time for the long swim.*

They left under the white heat of approaching summer and slowly, slowly, made their way northward. They came at last to a place where the water was cool. It was a long way still from the People's meeting place, but there were hard-backed creatures in abundance and many silver schools of water-breathers. Other tiny foods lived in the kelp and the eelgrass. For the first time in months the mother had enough to eat. The calf rested, and nursed, and rested again, and the mother thought she could see it grow stronger. She sang longingly to herself of her People away in the north, but even as she sang she knew she and the calf would go no farther.

With lazy, slow movements of her flukes, her baleen gentle as seaweed, she passed over the muddy ocean bottom. Her calf was lost to sight in the murk, though less than a body length away. She listened for it, hearing its contented body, its lack of needs. Sending it a bubble stream in warning, she surfaced, her spout whooshing into the sun. Air streamed endlessly into her great lungs. Like a tiny echo, the calf spouted beside her.

She rolled to one side, then the other, letting light glitter its visions into each half-closed, solitary eye. Landward there were high places, dark against the brightness. Higher still were flyers, almost too small to see, only the loudswift wing-noise identifying them. Other sounds: the barking yelp of small flippered ones speckling the dry places below the heights; tidewater hissing over the shelled backs of food creatures; the splashing, rippling roar of surf; the windpattern of this water and this land. Nearby was a seastack of stone, splashed by waves. She nudged the calf that way, then rubbed her body against the stone, trying to remove the barnacles that plagued her.

Rough, ah, good.

Beyond the stone lay smooth water. A bay. She squinted at it. The high places lining this bay were white as breaking waves. The water tasted of rust and rotting wood. The windsong was unmistakable.

Memory.

Her People knew this bay.

Her People had always known it.

They had known the bay when warmer waters had filled it, because long ago it had lain far to the south toward the calving place. In those days the Song had been a bare, undecorated melody of fog and storm and earthquake and sunlight, of feedings and birthings and dyings. As the ages passed and the Song's melody grew richer, this bay moved northward. It was a migration like the People's own, but slow and jerky, cataclysm caused. There was danger when the bay moved: waves that dwarfed even one of the People, maelstroms that sucked them in and fed on them, sounds that distorted the Song and sent the People mad.

But the bay was not going to move today. And this was a place the calf should know, a place where the Song had changed forever.

The mother dropped her head so that only her blowholes were in the air. The calf, observing, did likewise. And the mother sang, and the calf listened, and her memory became its own.

In the beginning, the Song sings, bright as the flashes of water-breathers in the deeps where few but we can see. We of the People listen to the Song and understand; we sing with the melody; we know what is and what is not. In this, we are alone.

Listen now, Calfling. Hear the Song change. See what I see, the coming of the air-breathers that move about on two legs and have no wings. See them gather food in the shallows with their not-flippers-not-paws. Listen to them! They do not hear us; perhaps they cannot, but their minds can sing like ours. And we of the People, we listen to their singing, and almost we understand. But, oh! Their songs are dark!

Deep from the layers of the People's memory the mother sang those songs. The calf listened as the unadorned, easy melody of the Song thickened, losing itself in counterpoint and odd, dark tonalities. It was like the muddying of clear water by feeding. Confused, the calf moved closer to its mother. But there was more: later harmonies winding about the first, the Song growing

18

stranger still, and darker. The calf nudged its mother anxiously, but she did not stop singing.

See, calfling, see the two logs, each with pale wings flapping like flyers entangled in eelgrass? There are two-legged ones inside those logs. It is how they swim, for they are small and have no flukes, and the sea is cold and big. See the two logs come into this bay?—see how the wings fold inward? Now the two-legged ones are lowering little logs over the sides of the big ones. Now, digging with sticks into the water, they are taking the little logs ashore.

And still the mother sang, and the Song grew darker and darker, and the calf lay quiet in the water and listened unblinking.

The big log is dragged into the shallows and lifted out of the water. Ah, they scrape the log's barnacles! Smell the stink of their hot fogs rising up into the sky! See their sharp things glitter, one against the other!

And then, darkest of all.

Sing with me, calfling, sing, for I am lonely.

CHAPTER TWO

"MARTY SAYS WE'RE GONNA SEE WATER soon. The Estero's behind that hill up ahead. Dad?"

Junie Niven squirmed her skinny nine-year-old body forward, trying to squeeze between the two front seats of the van. The hill she was pointing at was a rugged slope dotted with coyote bush and the fading purple of lupine. There were no animals grazing on it, though most of the other hills they had passed had cows pasted like cutouts onto their summits. The sky was a vivid blue, and the ditch a riot of yellow broom, but the grass on the hill was pale and parched looking, like straw.

Junie was prodding at her father's neck. "You said you were sick of dry rivers and dead grass. Yoohoo, Dad! Marty says there's water coming up!"

Marty Griffiths fingered the map self-consciously. She had muttered the thought to herself, not meaning anybody else to hear. Six-year-old Kathy was asleep, her head on Marty's lap, her mouth slightly open and snoring. And Junie had seemed engrossed in her crossword puzzle. But Junie always heard everything. It was something Marty had had to get used to in the three years since the school guidance office had found her this job baby-sitting the two Niven kids.

"Wake up, Sam," Lynda Niven told her husband. She took one hand off the steering wheel long enough to poke his shoulder. "Junie's talking to you."

"I wasn't asleep," Sam said with dignity. "Under torture

20

I could recite every word Junie has said since we left Petaluma. What was that about a hill, and water?" He peered out his window.

"Not that side, Dad! He's looking in the wrong direction. Left, Dad, not right. Left!"

Sam protested feebly. "Just loosening up my neck muscles. Left, you say. *That* hill? Hmm. Let's have that map."

"Must you?" Lynda said. "We'll be seeing around it with our own eyes in a minute. My money's on Marty, anyway, whatever you say."

"A challenge," Sam said calmly. "Marty, the map."

Marty handed it over. Sam looked at it, squinted at the hill again, and said confidently, "Too low."

"I'm probably wrong," Marty said quickly. If a professor from the University of British Columbia couldn't identify a hill after looking at a topographical map, how could she? And then they rounded the hill between slopes on the left and right, and when they came out into the open again there was marshland to the right and a stretch of muddy flats to the left, beyond which a snowy egret stood fishing in the pale, shallow waters of an estuary.

"Drake's Estero it is," Sam said, sketching a bow in Marty's direction. "An *A* for Miss Griffiths."

"I told you Marty knew," Junie said proudly. "She always knows where things are."

"A useful person to have around a household like ours," Lynda said.

Embarrassed, Marty looked down. All this praise for somebody who had barely passed the tenth grade! They didn't know, of course. She hadn't told them. In the three years she'd known them she had said very little about herself—or anything else, either. Sam and Lynda never seemed to notice how quiet she was. And she had really tried to join in, on this trip south from Vancouver to Point Reyes. But she had a soft voice, and a slow one, and every one of the Nivens was quick and clever and bad at

21

waiting. Jammed into the van with tents and bikes and diving gear and four talkative people, she had ended up silent as a lump while they commented and remarked and objected and argued. Lynda would say something about some news story on the radio and then Sam would purse his lips and say exactly why Lynda was wrong, and then Lyn would point out all the flaws in *his* argument, and Junie would disagree with both of them, and then Kathy would complain that everybody was using words she didn't know. And then the whole thing would stop and start off in a new direction as everybody tried to explain, because in this family, nothing was as important as words. And Marty would sit and listen like an observer at a tennis match, and sometimes she felt as if she were drowning in words and, sometimes, as if she were flying.

They were on a new tack now. "Funny to see so many radio receivers here," Lynda said, pointing to a maze of poles, dishes, and wires to the right of the road.

"Not just radio," Sam said. "Those are satellite dishes. Telecommunications stuff, I'll bet."

They were climbing now, the van laboring up a winding, steep road lined with rolling pastureland. The Estero came in and out of view. The higher they got, the more they could see of it. It was much bigger than it had seemed at first, an inland sea shaped like a four-fingered hand. Its "wrist" was a narrow channel joining the Pacific at Drake's Bay. From one spot high on the peninsula Marty could see the white rollers of Drake's Bay smashing into a sandbar beyond the Estero's mouth, while at the same time the land to the right of the road dropped precipitously away into pounding waves that had touched no land since Asia. Ocean to the left and ocean to the right: It was like being perched on the back of some huge sea-creature, about to dive. Marty hugged the thought to herself while Junie and her parents chattered.

They passed more of the fenced-off dairy farms, and

once even a school bus sign, but there were no people. At last the van overtook a couple of sweating backpackers who were photographing a red-tailed hawk sitting calmly on a fencepost. A short distance afterward, the road forked, and they took the branch to the left, marked by a sign for Drake's Bay. Junie said something about a drake being a male duck, and Sam and Lyn tried to give her a history lesson, but Marty barely listened.

They were descending, though still very high. Marty could see part of a parking lot far away at the bottom, and to the right of it, another hill, marked by a faint black line that might be a tarmac trail. There were splashes of color at the top; she thought they were tents. Beyond were heavily eroded white cliffs, sweeping an arc through the water to a far, rocky point. She let her eyes rest on that, but only for a moment. She felt as if she were looking for something.

"Kathy's still asleep," Junie said suddenly. "She'll be mad if she misses us getting there."

"Let her sleep," Sam said. "We don't want her grumping around while we're trying to set up camp."

"No child of mine would even think of grumping around in a place like Point Reyes," Lynda said. "Hiking and biking and archaeological digs and swimming—"

"Only on the Drake's Bay side," Sam reminded them. "Too dangerous to swim anywhere else."

"I'll bet you guys will scuba where you want," Junie said.

"Where we have to," Sam corrected her. He and Lynda were marine biologists and often had to dive for samples. "Scuba diving isn't like swimming, anyway. You can avoid the currents if you go far enough down."

"Is this the summer you're finally going to teach me?" Junie asked.

Lynda gave an exasperated sigh. "You may pretend not to recall this, Junie Niven, but your father and I are here

23

to *work*. So are all the other adults. There's to be no bothering the grown-ups this summer, young lady. It's you and Kathy and Marty against the world."

The road began to descend so sharply that Lynda slowed the van to a crawl. On their left, gnarled bushes hugged the cliff, rising more and more steeply over their heads. There was a hill to their right, too, though less sheer. The road tunneled between them. To the left at the bottom was the roof of some kind of building, nestled in evergreens. To the right was a small lake, very blue, surrounded by the browns and greens of marsh plants. Past the lake, the road ended in the parking lot, which they could now see in its entirety. It was huge and almost completely empty. Beyond that was beach and a brilliant, vast expanse of blue, glinting with light.

"Drake's Bay," Lynda said, stepping a little harder on the accelerator.

"The ends of the earth, you mean," Sam said, yawning. "I hope this campsite of ours isn't too far from the parking lot. We've got a lot to carry."

"The camp's up on the bluffs," Lyn said, scrabbling in her handbag with one hand. "Southwest of the parking lot, I think Ray said. You read it." She thrust a letter at him.

"There are some tents on the top of that hill over there," Marty said, pointing.

Sam groaned. The hill did seem very high.

"About that scuba diving," Junie said as Lyn steered the van into the parking lot. "Marty's getting weekends off, isn't she? That means you guys are going to have to spend time with Kathy and me—"

"We're not going to spend our free time teaching you to scuba!" Sam said. "Suiting up again on our evenings and weekends off is the last thing we'll want after spending the entire workweek in wet suits."

Junie scowled at her father. "Why bother being with

24

Kathy and me at all? I wish we could have Marty on the weekends too."

"Maybe there will be times we'll wish that too."

Marty was silent. She had offered half a dozen times already to look after the kids on the weekends, but Lynda wouldn't allow it. "We'd be carting you home on a stretcher before the summer was half over," Lyn always said. "And then what would we do with these two wretches of ours? It was touch and go getting permission to bring them at all. No, Marty. You need time off, and you're going to get it."

All those free hours, Marty thought now. No other kids her own age. No TV, no movies, and no town within miles. There'd be biking and swimming and wildlife to watch, but she'd be doing that all week with the two kids. Would she really want to spend her weekends alone and doing the same things?

Probably Lynda and Sam thought she'd read. That was what they would do. There wasn't a single room in their house, not even the bathroom, that wasn't piled with books. But Marty hadn't brought any books to read. She didn't own any; nobody in her family did. She wouldn't have spent her spare time reading, anyway. Reading wasn't fun to her. Reading was what she sweated over, school night after school night, trying to make things make sense and never more than half succeeding.

Fifty percent. A bare pass. How could somebody work so hard and get only fifty? And not just this year, but last year too. And the eleventh grade would be harder. Everybody said so. Why should she even bother to try?

She had turned sixteen in May. When you were sixteen, you could quit school.

And then what? she asked herself. Clerk at Safeway for the rest of her life, like her mother? Drink herself to sleep in front of the TV every night like her dad?

Time off to think, that was what Sam and Lynda were

giving her. Time off to think, to face what was wrong with her, to decide.

It was the last thing in the world that Marty wanted.

It was late in the afternoon when Nick climbed back up the path to the campsite. He had walked for hours, a swift, arm-swinging walk that took him past harbor seals splashing in the estuary, past herons wading on their sticklike legs, past flocks of fluffy sanderlings pecking up food in the brief moments between a wave's receding and its curling back shoreward. He saw none of it. Wherever he went, whether it was along the beach or high on the cliffs where the California poppies bloomed, or deeper inland on pale scrub dotted with coyote bush and monkey flower, his mind saw only that large white ship anchored so placidly in the bay.

There was no escaping it. Letting Dr. Anderson down, flying home to no job and no money and a summer full of arguments would be worse than staying. The *Leviathan* was in his mind now. He could see it with his eyes closed. He would keep on seeing it whether he was in Vancouver or here. He couldn't get away from it, just as he couldn't get away from the bits of Richard that were buried in a Vancouver graveyard.

Dr. Anderson was standing at the top of the tarmac trail, looking down toward Nick. There was a lot of noise and activity in the campsite behind him, the roar of gas jets under camp stoves, the rattle of pots, people shaking hands or passing things to one another or hammering tent pegs. But Dr. Anderson was motionless, waiting for Nick, his gray eyes very narrow.

When Nick got to the top he faced him. "I've decided to stay," he said. His voice was stiff, as if he hadn't used it for years.

Dr. Anderson made a big deal of getting out his pipe. He undid his tobacco pouch, filled his pipe, and lit it.

Between puffs he said, "I've been thinking about the laptop. I could recharge the batteries for you. Save you having to go out to the ship so often."

Staying meant doing it properly. The whole thing, even to rowing out to the *Leviathan* every day, even to nodding politely at Ray Pembroke, the man who'd taken Richard away from a perfectly safe academic career and turned him into one of those rabid protestors who were always being written up in the newspaper. Unknown mill workers angry at a shutdown brought on by Conservocean had planted the bomb that had blown Richard to pieces. But in Nick's eyes it was Ray Pembroke who had been responsible.

Nick raised his chin. "Thanks," he said, "but it's my job. I'll recharge the batteries."

"I thought you'd say that," Dr. Anderson said. That was all, but something tight and coiled relaxed in Nick, and he suddenly felt very tired.

"The only thing is," Nick muttered, "I don't want— that is, does Pembroke have to know who I am?"

"I haven't told him my assistant is his former student's brother. Pembroke spends most of his time out testing for chemicals along the coast, so you needn't run into him all that often. And Nick Young could be anybody's name."

Briefly the older man's hand rested on Nick's shoulder, then he turned casually and used that hand to point at the campsite. "Lots done since we got here," he said.

There had only been five tents in the camp when Nick had left: a small one isolated at the southwest end of the hilltop, the enormous dining tent at the nearer end, two low pup tents beside that for the administrator and the cook, and beside those, the one that would be shared by Nick and Dr. Anderson. But now across from the dining tent a couple of women were putting tent poles together for what looked like a wilderness tent. Another tent was already standing beside that. Its occupant came out while he looked, a gray-haired woman in a skirt and rubber boots, carrying a plastic bag full of cracker boxes. She went purposefully over to a man who was erecting a long T-shaped pole near the wooden railing that prevented people from going too near the edge of the bluffs. Two more tents, one of them big enough to have a bedroom compartment, stood at the far west side of the campsite, right beside the small tent that had been all on its own before.

Dr. Anderson nodded at that one. "Art Dunn likes things quiet," he said. "He'll be surprised when he comes back to find he's got a family with two little kids next door."

"Kids?" Nick said. "I thought—"

"Special permission," Dr. Anderson explained. "Sam and Lynda Niven are both marine biologists. From UBC, actually. Damn good ones, too, or so I hear. Wanted to come and didn't want to leave their kids. Solution: Bring a baby-sitter. That's the baby-sitter over there in the doorway of the Nivens' tent. See her? Girl with the hair, talking to the little kid."

Nick could see why Dr. Anderson singled out the baby-sitter's hair. It was the color of burned sugar, beautiful as stained glass. The girl was crouched down to be on the little kid's level, and her hair was so long it actually brushed the ground, now sweeping softly forward to enclose the two of them in its shadow, now sliding briefly to one side to expose the girl's profile. It was like a dance, Nick thought, fascinated, the girl's movement echoed by her hair's, two harmonies working together.

The baby-sitter's face, when he got around to looking at it, was not at all what Nick usually thought of as pretty. It was too white and bony, and too much of it seemed to be taken up by her large, dark eyes. She was listening to the little girl with a concentration that interested Nick. It was as if for that moment there was no one else in the world for her but the child.

"They pay attention to her," Dr. Anderson said.

"Sorry?" Nick blinked at him.

"The baby-sitter. Those kids pay attention to her." He grinned. "Not the only ones, it looks like."

The girl was standing up now. She was tall, almost as tall as Nick, and slender as a dancer. Even just standing still, there was an intensity to her. It reminded Nick of someone wearing earphones, listening to things no one else could hear. She would have seen Nick if she had lifted her eyes, but she didn't. The little girl said something. The baby-sitter reached out her hand to the child, who laughed audibly, avoided her hand, and tangled her fingers instead in the baby-sitter's hair. Then together they walked back into the big tent, letting the flap drop behind them.

Nick turned away. Dr. Anderson was puffing studiously at his pipe. "Ready to meet a few people?" he asked innocently. But his gray eyes were twinkling.

How long had be been looking at that girl, anyway? Nick shook his head. "I think I'll unpack first," he said gruffly.

"Go ahead, then," the older man replied. "Oh, by the way, don't leave any food in your tent, or the raccoons will be after it. Hang it from that pole over there." He pointed to the T-shaped pole standing between the dining tent and the wooden railing. The man who had been putting it up was now hanging the clear plastic bag of crackers from the crossbar. "That's Paul Wilson, our cook. Woman with him is Sheila Gough. American zoologist, specializes in invertebrates. But there'll be plenty of time for introductions later tonight. That baby-sitter, for instance—"

"I think I'll be figuring out the laptop tonight," Nick demurred. "You'll be wanting me to start real work tomorrow, won't you?"

29

"Good grief, Nick, I'm not a slave driver! You can have the night off!"

"But you did say you already had quite a bit of data. I don't want to hold you up."

"Suit yourself," Dr. Anderson replied, shrugging a little.

At least his eyes had stopped twinkling. That was something, Nick thought, stumping off toward his tent. Maybe there would be no more of those remarks about the baby-sitter.

There had better not be. Nick had enough to worry about this summer without people trying to pair him up with some girl.

CHAPTER THREE

IN THE DARK POINT REYES NIGHT, MARTY lay still. The tent smelled as musty and stale as old chalk erasers. The odor sent her back a long time, to a third-grade classroom in Vancouver on one particular Indian summer afternoon, shouts of children ringing outside and shafts of sun laden with chalk dust slanting across the small, ink-stained desks. She saw herself there, a skinny, pigtailed eight-year-old all alone in the room, cleaning the chalk erasers the way Mrs. Hayes had taught her, banging them one against the other and wiping them with a cloth and in between straining to catch the voices in the hall outside. The man was doing most of the talking. He was the same one who had taken Marty out of class last week, asking her a million questions and making her draw things and read aloud and describe something he'd covered with aluminum foil. Every time she answered he wrote stuff down, and his pen scrawled across the page so fast and hard it made her nervous. He underlined things, too. Now, talking to Mom and Mrs. Hayes, his voice was like his pen had been, coming out in quick, underlining bursts.

"—not ever going to read as well as—" came one loud rush of words. And then, "—highly advanced in other ways—sense of pattern—acute memory for visual and aural—" It seemed the big words would never stop.

"Then why?" It was Mrs. Hayes, crisp as usual, interrupting.

Another male torrent. "—That, no one's sure . . . left

31

hemisphere of the brain—" On and on. And finally, "Not your traditional learning disability. It wouldn't even *be* a disability, in a culture less verbal."

"Extra home practice wouldn't hurt, would it?" Mrs. Hayes again. "Reading aloud. She might not hate it so much if she did it at home. And what about bedtime stories? You do read to her regularly, don't you, Mrs. Griffiths?"

"I work nights," Mom said, her voice defensive. "And her father—well, Jim doesn't believe in fairy tales."

Later, the man had said good-bye to Marty. "Don't worry about being a bit slow at reading. Once you're out of school, no one will care. And don't go undervaluing what you do have, trying for something else. Remember the story of the Little Mermaid."

Marty didn't understand what he meant. She had never heard of the Little Mermaid. But then, a couple of weeks ago, she had taken Kathy and Junie to see the movie. It was about a mermaid who had given up the sea's freedom and lightness and even her own voice, just to become a human.

If it had been me, I wouldn't have, Marty thought.

She was tired, and it was very late. She bunched up her pillow and squirmed deeper into her sleeping bag, but images kept forming behind her eyelids. The dining tent tonight, crowded with people grabbing cutlery and plates and dumping themselves down at the camping tables. The cheerful meal of hamburgers and instant pudding and coffee. Kathy playing hide-and-seek among the tables, Junie sipping California wine from her mother's glass, the shadow that was Marty herself covering her plate with a paper towel, too wound up to eat. It was like watching a movie with herself as one of the characters and *being* the movie character at the same time. As if, she thought, she were two people at once, sharing a single pair of eyes.

The evening's events continued to unreel. Businesslike

Dr. Gough in smelly rubber boots calmly chewing her way through four large hamburgers. The Ph.D. student, Glenna Hoyt, fluttering like a moth around a man who talked in an uncomfortable voice about fluid dynamics. Nice Dr. Duguay, here to count marine mammals—"None of the gray whales that Point Reyes is famous for, not at this time of the year, but maybe we'll have an elephant seal or two to make up for it. And do call me Ann, Marty. There are too many doctors here as it is."

In the center of the tent was the photographer, Janet Simpson, who was camping in her van in the parking lot because she had too much valuable equipment to trust to a tent. She was explaining in her drawling voice why she called the people in the trailer parked next to her the FOGS. "It's for Fisheries, Ornithology, and Graduate Student. And I haven't the foggiest idea which of them is which."

Ewan Faulkner, Janet Simpson's Fisheries neighbor, was from San Francisco. Sam and Lynda had met him before, and he sat with them at dinner, talking excitedly about things like plankton and sedimentation rate. The man who was Ornithology had an open notebook beside his hamburger and kept writing things down as he ate. The Graduate Student was wearing a pair of cutoffs and a shirt open to his navel. The administrative officer, Heather Kent, kept trying to make conversation with him, but he was spending the evening taking apart a pair of binoculars and mostly ignored her.

There were two more people in the dining tent. They were at the far end, some distance from where Marty sat. Sharp-eyed, stocky Jonas Anderson had introduced himself to Sam and Lynda before dinner. The boy with him wasn't exactly a boy; he was too old for that. But he wasn't a man yet, either. He was as tall as a man, but his feet and hands were too big for his body, like a puppy whose paws announce that it has a long way still to grow.

33

His shoulders were wide but a little too thin, and he kept them hunched forward, as if to protect himself. He had come in late, not greeting anybody, and all through the meal he looked only at his plate or at Dr. Anderson. He ate very little. He had dark hair, short except at the front, and whenever it fell over his forehead his hands would brush it away, thin and impatient.

As soon as dessert was over, the boy got up to leave. While passing Marty's table, his dark blue eyes met hers, and Marty knew at once that he hadn't wanted to let that happen. He hadn't wanted to acknowledge her at all. He's angry, Marty told herself. And then, Why is he angry at me?

A few minutes later some more people came in. They were from the ship anchored in Drake's Bay. "Part of the Conservocean gang," Sam told Marty. "That's the foundation that organized this field trip. They're hoping this summer's research will persuade the government to extend the existing marine sanctuary."

The man at the front of this new group had a deeply tanned face and an attractive, lopsided smile. He wore jeans so old they were almost white. His windblown hair was mostly brown, but the sun had done strange things to it, lightening it without making it blond, revealing odd hints of green. He stood chatting with Heather Kent for a minute or two, but rarely looked at her. Instead his eyes made rapid journeys around the dining tent. Like someone checking off a list, Marty thought. His hair and his hazel eyes matched almost exactly.

"That's Ray Pembroke," Sam said. "He's the head of Conservocean. A chemical oceanographer by training, but his real genius is fund-raising. One of the most focused men I've ever met. The West Coast owes him a big debt."

"There are some unemployed people in Seattle who wouldn't agree," Lyn put in. She explained to Marty, "Ray got one of the biggest paper mills there closed down for breaking environmental laws."

After a while, Pembroke began going from table to table. He seemed to know almost everyone. When he got to the Nivens, he shook hands with Marty, patted Kathy's dark curls, and tried for Junie, who ducked. "Glad to have you with us," he told the three girls, and sounded as if he really meant it. His wife was beside him, darkly good-looking despite the long lines around her mouth. The other newcomers with them—two youngish women and a scuba diver named Bill Lancaster—all seemed to like Pembroke. So did the scientists in the camp. But Marty wasn't sure.

Over the rest of evening she watched him, idly at first, then more intently. His easy smile so carefully matched by his crinkling eyes, his light voice laughing, his tanned, muscular arm draped casually around his wife's shoulders, were all so different from that impatiently jerking muscle in his neck and his strong fingers that occasionally drummed out a powerful rhythm on a table. He had a way of putting down his beer mug in exactly the same spot it had been before, the handle turned just so, which was as controlled and aware as anything Marty had ever seen in her life. Once she had noticed it, she couldn't stop looking for it. She watched in fascination so many times that it wasn't surprising he finally caught her at it. He looked at her, his fingers stroking the handle, and gave her a brilliant, amused grin, then deliberately turned the handle away. She blushed, but he had already gone back to Heather Kent. A moment later, when Marty dared to look again, the handle was back at the angle it had been before.

The memories stopped. Darkness weighed down on Point Reyes, on Marty. She closed her eyes. The sleeping bag was warm and soft. The outside world, heavy with night, was shut away. The distant surf sang in Marty's mind like a lullaby.

In the sea, it was the land that was dangerous. Hidden shoals, watery sandbars, reefs like teeth—these were the things the seafarer feared. Fog, obscuring all boundaries. Beaching.

Marty's shallow breathing deepened. She was swimming. The water was bitterly cold. She recognized the cold but was at home in it. Above her head the moonlight glittered. She rested her eyes by looking down. Infinite darkness. The delicate touch of kelp. Surf gentle against her body. Peace.

Sleep, calfling, for I am here. Sleep.

She slept.

When Marty opened her eyes, dim gray light was filtering into her tent. For a moment she blinked into it, then she knew. Camping. Point Reyes. Baby-sitting. She looked at her watch. It was only five-thirty. In the big tent next door Junie and Kathy would be sound asleep. They'd sleep for another two hours, or maybe three, after their late night last night.

Quickly she unzipped her sleeping bag, got dressed, grabbed her toothbrush and washcloth, and crawled out of her tent. It was still very early, and she was the only one up. The morning was glorious. Marty breathed in deep drafts of the cool sea air, turning her face to the sun rising over the hills of Inverness Ridge. The sky above was a vivid violet blue, the white cliffs below tinged with purple. Drake's Bay was in two parts, a narrow band of sandy shallows separated from the darker blue of deeper water by a line of surf. She could hear the waves when she listened for them. They made a deep, continuous rumble, dulled by distance and the wind. Inland, by the lake that lay to the north of the parking lot, she saw something move. Was it a deer? Yes! She strained her eyes. There was another deer with it, smaller than the first. A fawn!

The washrooms were in the Visitors' Center. After

36

finishing inside, she looked around the common court-yard. One of the walls was hung with panels that described Sir Francis Drake's visit in 1579. She began to read, slowly and carefully. Supposedly Drake had spent thirty-six days in Point Reyes. Before he got here, he had killed one of his best friends. He had taken communion with the condemned man, eaten a hearty meal with him, and then chopped off his head.

A hearty meal. Marty tried to imagine it. She wondered if the other man had eaten heartily, too.

"He had a brother," came a voice from behind her.

She turned. It was the boy from last night, the one with the blue eyes. His eyes were even angrier this morning. "Who had a brother?" she asked.

"Thomas Doughty," the boy said. "The man Drake killed. His brother, John Doughty, was with them on the voyage. John wasn't allowed to transfer to another ship after Drake executed his brother. Drake made John stay with him. He gloated over him all the way across the Pacific, around Africa, and back home to England."

Marty was silent, her head on one side, studying the boy.

"Drake made a no-fighting rule on board the *Golden Hind*, but if somebody broke it to attack John, that was okay. Whoever started the fight, it would be John he would end up punishing."

Still Marty was silent. The boy's anger surprised her. It was as if he had a personal reason to stand up for that other boy, that John Doughty.

"Drake tortured people. Keel-hauled them, or dangled them overboard till they almost drowned, then hauled them up, tied them to the mast, and read the Bible to them."

Marty frowned. "But Drake's a hero," she protested. "Look at all this stuff." She indicated the large panels featuring Drake.

37

The boy made a disgusted sound. "Some hero. He took a black woman prisoner on his way here. When she got too pregnant to be any further use he abandoned her on an uninhabited, waterless island near Java. And he excommunicated his own priest for saying Drake was wrong for killing Doughty."

"What happened to that boy in the end? The one whose brother Drake killed?"

"When they finally got back to England, John tried to get Drake prosecuted for murder. Drake, of course, had just brought home enough gold and silver to fix up England's economy for years. So John went to jail. Nobody ever heard of him again. A man kills your brother, and *you* rot in jail while the killer gets off."

Marty stared at him. He wasn't just angry, this boy, he was furious. Why did something that had happened more than four hundred years ago matter so much to him?

The boy saw her surprise and flushed. "Look at this place," he said defensively. "Drake this and Drake that, making a big thing out of a jerk like that, and to hell with the truth. It's just one more example." He stopped abruptly. When Marty didn't answer, he lifted his chin defiantly. "I suppose you don't believe me. Well, I read a book about it this morning. The definitive book on the subject, Dr. Anderson called it. Everything I told you was in it. Drake wasn't a hero. He was an opportunist and he was a sailor and he was a killer, but he wasn't a hero."

"What's your name?"

"Nick. Nick Young." He brushed awkwardly at a lock of hair that had fallen over his forehead.

"I'm Marty."

"I know. I heard the little kids call you that. You're their baby-sitter, aren't you? I'm Dr. Anderson's research assistant."

Her long hair slid forward to hide her face. Research

assistant. You had to be pretty smart to be something like that.

There was a short silence. Then Nick said stiffly, "Well, I've got things to do."

She raised her eyes about halfway up his chest. "I should go, too. I'm not really in charge of the kids till after breakfast, but—"

"See you around, then."

"Yeah, see you." But if he heard, he made no sign. He was already striding off toward the camp.

The same direction she was going, Marty thought. They could have walked up together, but obviously he didn't want to.

CHAPTER FOUR

SOUTHWEST BEYOND THE CAMP THERE was a clear trail along the bluffs, heading in the general direction of Chimney Rock. At breakfast they talked about following it. "It's a lot farther than it looks," Sam warned, "and those things up there in the fields look like bulls to me."

"You don't want to overdo it, your first day," Lyn added. "Sore muscles for a week is no way to start the summer."

In the end, though, it was Junie who decided it. "We're not tourists," she said, "we're explorers. We'll go the other way, and we'll make our own trails."

By the time they were ready, backpacks crammed with compass and bird book and maps and swimming things and beach toys and picnic lunches, the camp was nearly empty. Sam and Lynda were already gone, driving off with Ewan Faulkner to a beach where he'd discovered an underwater kelp forest. Dr. Anderson's car was the only one left in the parking lot. He was standing beside it, giving some instructions to Nick, who had his eyes so carefully fastened on the older man's face that he didn't seem to notice the three girls walk by. He didn't turn even when Dr. Anderson called out, "You three know today's tides?"

"High tide's at four o'clock, isn't it?" Marty asked. "That was what was marked on the board at the Visitors' Center."

"That board's nearly always out of date," Dr. Anderson

said, fumbling in his pocket and pulling out a booklet. He left Nick's side and walked over to her, leafing through the booklet as he went. "Here we are. Monday, June twenty-sixth." He held it out, showing Marty a page blindingly full of numbers. "You have to subtract to get the right time for Point Reyes. The middle pages tell you the correction factor. See? So today's high tide"—he paused, calculating—"is at five-thirty, or near enough. Got it?"

"Five-thirty." Marty repeated. Not for anything would she admit she had no idea how he'd figured it out. Not with Nick so near.

"Here, you keep the booklet," Dr. Anderson said. "I can get another."

He hurried off and rejoined Nick, who still didn't bother noticing the three girls. Marty straightened her shoulders. "Let's hurry," she urged. "Exploring doesn't start till we're out of the parking lot."

It was a tough climb up to the bluffs behind the Visitors' Center. Now facing into the cheesy white soil of the cliff itself, now twisting back on themselves, they climbed up and up, getting new views each time of the beach and the campsite on the bluffs across the way. A little stream angled over the beach to a point directly below them. Here the stream had hollowed out a small inlet in the cliff before turning toward the bay. This inlet was where Conservocean beached the rowboats used by the scientists of the camp. Marty looked down on one now, small as a toy. Then they were up on top of the bluffs, where the wind blew hard and free.

It was a much rougher world up here, the grass long and twisted, the tough stalks catching their feet and hiding the ankle-turning pits of old hoof marks dried like fossils in the clay. There were cowpats to watch out for as well, and the sharp barbs of milk thistle. When, deeper inland, they came upon a two-lane dirt track heading downhill toward a large pond, they followed it along the pond and then up the hill on the other side. The sun was hot and the wind cold. They puffed and sweated as they climbed.

"This is no good," Marty said after a while. They were high on a treeless upland, but not high enough to see past the hills humped all around them. "Let's leave the trail. It goes forever."

They didn't care which way they went, and so they followed a hummingbird. It stopped often, and so did they, watching it sip daintily at one monkey-flower bush after another. They soon lost sight of the trail. On that empty, rolling grassland, with no landmarks for Junie to use her new compass on, Marty supposed she should have been worried about getting lost. But for some reason, whether it was the direction of the wind or the look of the sky, she always knew where Drake's Bay was.

Around noon they reached a steep descent overlooking a large body of water. "It's the Estero," Marty said.

"It can't be," Junie protested. "We've come much farther than that."

"Up and down makes everything farther," Marty said.

"But it doesn't look a bit like the Estero we saw from the road. That was like a hand with four fingers. This isn't like that at all."

"On the road we were higher up, so we could see the whole hand. Here we're too close to it. But I'm sure that's the wrist." She pointed ahead and to the right, to the channel at the end of a long spit of sand separating the inland waterway from the surf of Drake's Bay.

"I'll check it with my compass," Junie said.

She began rooting in her backpack, while Marty looked down at a small, marshy pond immediately below them. It was very close to the Estero, so close that it had probably been part of it once. Now it was separated from the larger body of water by a cow fence and a narrow strip of grassy sand dunes. On the dunes, about halfway between the little pond and the Estero, a tall post had been erected. A sign was posted on it, impossible to read at this distance.

A moving patch of white at the nearer side of the pond caught Marty's eyes. She touched Kathy's elbow and whispered, "An egret. Look, he's hunting for his dinner."

"I'm hungrier than he is, I bet," Kathy declared.

"You're always hungry," her sister said impatiently.

"Well, I am. And I'm thirsty. And my backpack's hurting me. And my head's hot and the rest of me's cold and my legs—"

"It's too windy up here for a picnic," Marty said. "Let's head for the beach down there and have our lunch. We could swim in the Estero, afterward."

"Just let me take this reading," Junie said.

It was no use hurrying her. Marty got an apple out of her backpack and gave it to Kathy. While Kathy chewed and Junie squinted along the compass, Marty watched the Estero, silky smooth and ribboned with the wake of swimming ducks. She wanted to go down there. She wanted it so much that she was almost afraid to go.

"I'll draw the sight lines later," Junie said at last, scribbling on the back of her hand with a ballpoint pen.

They followed the top of the cliff for a little while, trying to find a spot where they could descend. To their surprise, they met the two-lane track they had abandoned earlier that morning. It branched here, the main part continuing its placid route along the uplands, the smaller, less important side route angling down to the Estero. They descended very rapidly, the path zigzagging around jutting bits of cliff. At the bottom they climbed the cow fence and hurried out onto the beach beyond. There, they stopped. After a morning of not knowing where they were going or why, they had found their destination.

They were standing almost at the edge of a little cove. It was a perfect bite: water into land; the land a ripple of

43

hard mud flats, the water tawny and impenetrable and absolutely smooth. To their left was the front part of the cliff they had scrambled down, jutting some distance into the water before cutting away backward to make a rounded edge for the cove. At their backs, invisible behind sand dunes tufted with beach grass and purple sea rocket, was the marshy pond. To their right, the other edge of the cove was marked by the sandy ridge that separated the inland Estero from the open waters of Drake's Bay. At the end near the channel the ridge was so flat Marty could see the bay beyond, with its lines of rollers smashing noiselessly onto the beach.

All around them was a maze of three-toed and webbed trails. There were wormholes, clam hills, lines of washed-up eelgrass, a few starfish, some kelp. There was not a single human footprint. A little way out on the water a loon floated, black head nodding; a grebe opened and shut its beak, swallowed, and swam lazily away. The sun poured down, golden and hot. It glistened on the backs of harbor seals lying like logs on a sandbar out beyond the cove, and silvered the water between. Away across its mirrored surface, they could see a herd of white deer grazing the high hills. Protected from the wind, everything was so still they could hear bees humming around some distant lupines and even smell the sweet lupine scent. They might have been the only three people in the world.

"It's a magic place," Kathy said.

While they ate lunch, and afterward, they watched the birds. Marty had never seen so many kinds. There were herons and plovers, willets and terns and ducks. Only Junie knew their names. Armed with her field guide she would ask Marty questions about beak color and plumage. "Is that salmon orange or yellow orange?" she would say, and Kathy and Marty would creep up on the birds, trying to get close enough to tell. When Kathy got bored with this, they went swimming. The cool, salty water first prickled against their hot skin and then soothed it. Marty's hair drifted like eelgrass in the currents. She could have stayed in the water all day, but too soon Kathy began flapping her arms like wings. "You're a mommy sea gull," she said to Marty, "and I'm your hungry baby."

Marty had made up such plays for Kathy ever since she'd known her. She had started it instead of telling stories, because she didn't know very many by heart and was ashamed to read aloud. The plays were full of action and had almost no words, and in the beginning Marty had acted out all the roles. But now Kathy and she each took parts. Today, after the sea gull, Kathy became a snowy egret sprinting about in the shallow water while Marty was the fish trying to escape her; and then Kathy, squirming her way into a sand dune, was a legless black lizard suddenly catching sight of Marty the hawk.

They explored a little then. Junie wanted to see what the sign on the post said, but Marty and Kathy were more interested in the pond. They left Junie, found a muddy streambed, and followed it to the place where it drained out of the pond, but there was no way to go farther without climbing the cow fence.

"You'd need hip boots, anyway," Marty said. "The mud's so—"

She was interrupted by a yell from Junie. "Marty, Kathy! It's about Drake. Come see!"

She was standing in front of the post, half lost in the lupine. They scrambled to join her. There was a big anchor leaning against the post. "See?" Junie pointed excitedly to the sign and read, " 'June 17, 1579. Francis Drake landed in this cove and here repaired his ship the *Golden Hind.*' It was here, Marty!"

"Who's Francis Drake?" Kathy asked.

Junie explained. Kathy's eyes grew round. "And is that *his* anchor?"

"No, silly. It's a monument. They put it here to show people, that's all."

"I think it *was* his anchor. I think he lost it off his ship and it fell in the water and—"

"It's more than four hundred years since he was here. If it had been Drake's real anchor, it'd have rusted to bits."

Kathy's jaw went out. "He was a pirate, you said. A pirate anchor's special. They don't rust to bits. They—"

Marty stopped listening. Drake had anchored here, right here on this land that had once been water. In her mind she could see it so easily, the *Golden Hind* at anchor, noisy with too many men, the cooking smells, the natives on the hills watching in wonder. That boy, John Doughty, standing in the bow, hating Drake, hating him . . .

Keer, keer!

The gull's cry, almost in Marty's ear, made her jump. She looked around, frowning. The girls were no longer beside her. She pushed her way through the lupine, then ran back down to the beach. To her relief she saw the girls not too far away, heading for a rock shelf at the foot of the cliff they had climbed down earlier.

"Where are you going?" Marty called.

"Tide pooling," Junie called back, "we told you!" And as Marty ran up, "Come on, Kathy, I was first. No fair grabbing all the shells before I even get to see them."

Nick spent the entire day with the laptop, coming out of his tent only for lunch. Paul Wilson was peeling potatoes in front of the dining tent. "If you want something to eat, you'll have to help yourself," he told Nick cheerfully. He gestured over his shoulder to a table spread with breads, salad, and various kinds of cheese. "Most of the scientists don't want to waste time coming back to camp for lunch," Paul added, "so they make something in the morning to take with them."

There were only a few people eating inside the dining

tent. Marty wasn't one of them. Nick told himself he was glad. He remembered the burned-sugar gleam of her hair, the smell of her soap, her eyes, so big and questioning. What had gotten into him, to rave about Drake like that? She must think he was crazy.

Nick made himself a sandwich, then took it down to one of the picnic tables at the Visitors' Center. He bought a cup of coffee from the little restaurant inside, but forgot about it after one sip, staring out at Drake's Bay. Behind the line of surf the water was glassy, with no sign of waves. Yet at the shore the rollers raced in as if they had been whipped up by a storm. All that thunder and froth, all that splashing and hissing and boiling. Where did it come from?

He poured his coffee onto the ground and went back to his own tent. Dr. Anderson was out measuring rocks on the other side of Point Reyes. Already there were five lined pads full of numbers that needed to be transferred to disk. On the drive from the airport yesterday Dr. Anderson had wondered if it would be possible to get some computer graphics of the eroded surfaces he was interested in. There was no preprogrammed software package that would do exactly what Dr. Anderson wanted, but Nick hadn't given up on the idea. All the time he was entering data into storage, he was wondering if he could write a very specific graphics program of his own. The trouble was, he didn't know if he fully understood what all Dr. Anderson's measurements actually stood for. By the time the second battery pack had warned him it was wearing out, Nick had decided to go out and watch Dr. Anderson take measurements sometime in the next couple of days. He was going to have to learn it all, anyway, because he would be taking measurements himself whenever he didn't have enough to do on the computer.

He felt tired, but it was a good kind of tired. Nothing to think about but the screen and the numbers and the flowcharts and the problem. Even if it was a big, difficult problem, you always knew that in the end there would be a solution. All you had to do was work at it.

The worst part of his day lay ahead. He was going to have to row out to the *Leviathan* to recharge those batteries.

It was late in the day, and the weather was changing. The brilliant sun that had warmed the Estero all afternoon had turned a murky yellow, half covered by cloud. It was colder, too, and the air smelled dank. All the color had gone out of the water. Marty frowned up at the sky, absentmindedly fingering the clam shell Kathy had given her.

"The closed ones are almost always still alive," she said. "We can't keep this, Kathy. Why don't you put it back near the water?"

"You could eat it," Junie suggested.

Kathy's round little face got indignant. "I'm not gonna eat a live—"

"Better put on your sweats," Marty told the two children, wriggling into her own. "Get everything else into the backpacks. I don't like the look of the weather."

"Look at the dowitcher digging for food," Junie said. "Clams, probably," she added meanly to her sister.

White fingers of fog were drifting in from the bay. Marty eyed the bluffs. Already they were dimmer. That track would take them only partway home. And those pathless highlands, unfenced and dropping sheer to the sea, would be very dangerous for people who couldn't see where they were going. She looked at her watch: still an hour and a half before high tide. As long as they wasted no time, they could get back along the Drake's Bay Beach without being caught between the incoming water and those hard-to-climb cliffs. And it would be much safer on the beach, even with the tide coming in, than on those uplands in a fog.

She made up her mind. "We're going back along the beach. Here, Kathy, put your shells into my backpack."

"Race you to Drake's!" Junie called, bounding off along the mud flats beside the shallow estuary water. Kathy leaped after her. Chubby, barely half the gangly height of her older sister, and with shoelaces that invariably came undone, Kathy always lost the races she had with Junie. Then she would stamp her feet and make excuses and be miserable, but the next time there she'd be, racing again.

"Dumb," Junie called it.

"Too competitive for her own good," said her mother.

"Too young to calculate the odds," said her father.

But Marty didn't think it was any of those things that made Kathy run race after race when she always lost. Kathy knew she was going to lose, but she had to try. That was all it was. Kathy just had to try.

Marty kept pace with the little girl now, not outrunning her, but not wanting to lose sight of Junie, either. It was getting harder to see. In the distance, shapes were merging, blending with the fog and with each other. Worriedly, Marty looked down at Kathy, who was chugging along, elbows out and puffing. She was doing her best, but it was such a long way back to camp! And the weather was definitely worsening. A low-pitched, plaintive birdcall came out of the mist blanketing the water to her left. *O-wee-ah, o-wee-ah.* Marty shivered as she ran.

"Don't go over the sand dunes," she called to Junie. "Keep by the water, or you might get lost."

Junie stopped and looked back. "Slowpokes," she called cheerfully. Tendrils of fog surrounded her. A strand of her brown hair clung damply to her face. Her cheeks were flushed, and her eyes sparkled even through the mist. She looked very young. Then she was off once more. Suddenly and urgently, Marty wanted her back. She opened her mouth to call out, but her eye was caught by something at the mouth of the Estero.

Movement. Shapes, black shapes, moving in a sea of fog.

There was a two-legged one nearby.

The mother turned sharply in the water, mud and weed straining from her baleen. She knew that strange, warm scent. She vibrated a deep note of warning to her calf, but neither swam away. The two-legged ones here did not kill the People anymore. They killed only each other.

This one was full-grown, small and quick and agile. A male, the mother guessed. But for patches of white skin here and there, its body was covered in black, like orca hide. It did not see her in the thick murk. It was swimming underwater using flippers: unnatural smelling, not-alive-not-dead. It breathed oddly, never surfacing, yet with a pulsating stream of bubbles rising from it. It was a loud thing—breath bubbling, flippers thrashing, heart pounding with strain. Its mind sang in the way of a calf that has had enough milk, yet wants more. Greedy.

She watched it, now with one great eye, now with the other, following it but keeping her distance. The calf was an anxious shadow beside her. The two-legged one's forelimbs pointed straight ahead, something rigid sided and odd between them. The mother cast a vibration at the thing, analyzing the echo. It was like nothing she had ever known. It had the tingling kind of life possessed by some deepwater creatures, yet it was not alive and had never been alive. And certainly it sang no song.

The two-legged one had stopped swimming. Its breathing was quicker, its heart thudding harder and faster. Both forelimbs let go of the rigid thing, letting it dangle at the end of what looked like a strand of seaweed attached to its body. With both of its not-flippers-not-paws it gathered something up off the bottom. It rubbed the object against its black body, then held it in front of its strangely covered, close-set eyes.

A long, slow breath. Heartbeat steadying. Frustration, mingling with pleasure. Not what had been hoped for, after all. But close. Close.

And the mother knew, whatever it was that this two-legged one was greedy for, it was not milk.

CHAPTER FIVE

"JUNIE, COME BACK!"

Marty's voice came out half strangled. Junie stopped so quickly she almost fell. She turned, saw Marty's face, and cast a swift glance over her shoulder. Then, without a word, she ran back to them.

There was nothing to see. The narrow channel linking the Estero to the bay had disappeared, curtained off by fog. The black and white shapes had vanished as if they had never been there at all. Maybe they hadn't. Nothing could be relied on in a fog. A real pea-souper could muffle nearby sounds while making faraway ones seem right next door. Probably it was the same with shapes. Marty opened her clenched fist to take Kathy's clutching hand, but she couldn't stop herself from peering into the fog.

"What are you looking at, Marty?" Kathy, too, was staring hard. "I don't see anything. What are you looking at?"

"There's nothing there," Junie said. But her protest rang hollow, and she stood very close to Marty.

There was no wind. If there was any surf, Marty couldn't hear it. Her own heartbeat seemed loud to her. She stared and stared, silent in the murk.

Noisy things, not alive, not dead. Danger. Danger.

Like washing taking phantom shape on a clothesline, the fog suddenly rolled toward them, thick, gray billows with blurry edges and the odor of fish. Sounds and sights came and went within it: things swimming as if through a distorting lens, the cavernous clang of metal on metal, black and white shapes flickering, an echo like distant singing. Were those voices, out there? Marty strained her ears, but the words, if they had been words, were gone. The odd thing was that listening hard somehow made it easier to see. It was another trick of the fog. The less you looked, the more you saw. Studiously listening, Marty caught sight of the black and white shapes again.

"Marty?" Junie said. She sounded like a very little girl.

All at once Marty knew what she was seeing. The black and white shapes were just people, a couple of scuba divers in black wet suits. It was the suits that had thrown her, it must have been, making her think of something alien, black and white patches and a perpetual close-mouthed smile. They were wading out of the water. Now that she knew, it was easier to see them. What on earth had gotten into her?

One of the men was stripping off his air tank. Marty saw him—a still photo, blurry—then lost him again. The other she didn't see again. But she could hear him. His voice trickled against her ears. Mostly it was just rhythm, the words indistinguishable, though now and then whole sentences came sharply. Marty heard, "—Not like the one we found out in the bay, but—" and then, very distinctly, "Hand me that magnetometer, will you?"

"I heard that," Junie got out, her voice scared. "There's somebody there, isn't there?"

"They're just scuba divers, Junie," Marty said. "Nothing to worry about."

"Scuba divers!" Junie was furious. Marty knew it was because she had been frightened. "Is that all? Just scuba divers?"

The divers had heard. Out by the channel there was a whispered consultation, then a clanking sound and the rubbery flap of swim fins. A man materialized out of the fog and walked toward them. Only his wet suit stood out distinctly: a concise black, arms swinging great arcs through the fog, legs striding forward. The white parts of him—hands, feet, face—seemed blurry and odd, so that he was almost within touching distance before Marty recognized him. "Everything all right?" he asked.

"Fine, Dr. Pembroke," Marty answered him. Stupid, how high her voice came out. "We're just on our way back to camp."

"You're not lost, are you?"

"No, we—"

"What's a magnomer?" Kathy asked suddenly.

"A what?"

"She means *magnetometer*," Junie said, still angry. "You said it, a minute ago. 'Hand me that magnetometer.' We heard you."

Pembroke's eyebrows rose, making his black scuba helmet wrinkle. He seemed uncertain. Then his lopsided grin flashed. "A strange place for a science lesson," he said, "but who am I to stifle the curiosity of the young? A magnetometer is one of the instruments that Bill Lancaster and I use to find pollutants in the water. That's our study here this summer. Now, I think maybe you three should—"

"How come it's got the word *magnet* in it if it measures water pollution?" Junie asked, even more belligerently. The word *young* had acted on her as Marty could have predicted it would.

"We're looking for heavy metals," Pembroke explained, after a pause, "because they are some of the most deadly pollutants there are. Heavy metals can be magnetized, which means we can find them with the magnetometer. I'm afraid that's the best explanation I can give you. Now, I really do think you three should be on your way."

"Will we have time to get back along the beach before high tide?" Marty asked.

"A half hour to spare, as long as you don't build any

54

sand castles along the way. Keep to the shoreline and the fog won't confuse you."

"Won't it confuse *you*?" Junie asked, sticking her chin out.

"What—? Oh, I see. You're worried how we'll get back to the *Leviathan*. I don't think we'll attempt it tonight. Bill and I will hike back to camp and bunk in with somebody for the night. I won't offer to leave with you right this minute, though. We have a few things to finish up. I suppose you could wait for us, but the little ones might be a bit too slow to keep up with the speed we'll have to go then. You'll be perfectly safe on your own anyway, as long as you leave now."

"Little ones!" Junie hissed, half under her breath.

Marty took Junie's arm, felt the resistance in it, and tugged. "Thanks, Dr. Pembroke, we'll go right away. Come on, Junie. Kathy, hold my hand."

Marty could feel his eyes on her back, even when the fog had rolled in between them. When they had left the Estero behind and were out beside Drake's Bay, Junie exploded. "Sand castles? How old does he think we are? Sand castles!"

"Shh," Marty hissed, pointing.

Pulled up on the shore just ahead was a rubber dinghy. A wet-suited man, almost certainly Pembroke's associate, Bill Lancaster, was putting something into the dinghy. The fog was too thick for Marty to see the object clearly, but it must have been heavy, for Bill was grunting as he moved it. The fog cleared a little, and Marty caught a brief glimpse of the object before it disappeared into the bottom of the dinghy.

It was oddly shaped, and somehow didn't seem like scientific equipment. And she would have bet a day's pay it wasn't a water sample, either.

"Let's go and look," Junie whispered.

"Who's that?" the man called suddenly, and then,

55

seeing them, "Clear off, you kids. Expensive equipment here."

Marty shook her head at the two girls. They circled the boat to the right, saying nothing at all. Then they found the shoreline again and hurried on.

Fog, soaking and cold and impenetrable as cotton wool, blanketed Drake's Bay. On the foredeck of the *Leviathan*, Nick chewed his lip worriedly and squinted at the shore. He could only just see the notch in the cliffs that marked Drake's Beach and the Visitors' Center.

"You're not going to row back in this stuff, are you?" a sailor asked him.

Nick hesitated. It did look pretty bad. "How long will the fog last, do you think?"

"Maybe all night, and maybe all week," was the cheerful reply. "Better stay here, buddy. Only one life, huh?"

All week! Nick groaned to himself.

He had rowed out here; he had actually gone on board; the two battery packs he had used up today were plugged in and recharging; and today's work had been copied onto the hard disk of the ship's computer. He hadn't been able to make himself check the sleeping quarters of the ship to see if any sign of the bomb still remained. But he'd done what he'd come here to do. He'd done his job. He couldn't wait to be gone, and now someone was telling him he ought to stay on board.

Nick's stomach churned. The only thing that had made this first visit to the *Leviathan* bearable was that Ray Pembroke was away from the ship, collecting water samples. But out on the water Pembroke would have been sure to have seen the fog rolling in. Almost certainly he would be on his way back to the ship right now. If Nick stayed, and the fog really socked in, there would be no way to avoid him. Nick tried to imagine it, being shown around the ship by his polite host, making stilted dinner conversation, trying to answer Pembroke's questions without mentioning Richard's name. And never able to get away; nowhere to go that Richard had not gone too; nowhere to be alone.

"I'm not waiting," Nick told the sailor roughly. "I can still see the shoreline. If I hurry, I'll be all right."

Quickly he began climbing down the ladder that hung from the side of the *Leviathan*. Beads of fog had condensed on the metal rungs, making them slippery, but Nick didn't slow down. Even when he was safely inside the rowboat, he couldn't seem to stop hurrying. Impatiently, he untied the painter, then disentangled his oars from the larger ship's anchor line. When he began to row, for a while he didn't even look over his shoulder to see where he was going. Instead, he watched the *Leviathan* slowly dematerialize in front of him, its clean white lines blending into the fog that claimed it. That should have made it seem smaller to Nick, and less important, but somehow it didn't. It was as if, by blurring the ship's boundaries, the fog had actually made the *Leviathan* bigger. Nick dug the oars in, making more noise than he needed to counteract the silence everywhere else.

Nothing to be done. A man kills your brother, and nothing to be done.

When Nick could no longer be sure he was seeing the *Leviathan* at all, he maneuvered the rowboat around, deciding to backwater to shore. But now even the hazy view of the shore he had had from the *Leviathan*'s deck was gone, white cliffs blending into mist and silence. The rowboat alone was visible, the rest of the world curtained away inside a thick circle of white.

"Can you believe it?" Junie grumbled at supper. "People going away for a whole summer and not bringing a dictionary?"

"*You* didn't bring one," Marty said reasonably, passing

57

her a bowl of chowder. In another corner of the tent, Ray Pembroke was speaking quietly to Bill Lancaster, who watched him over the rim of his beer mug and said very little.

"What's the problem?" Sam said. With one hand he ruffled Junie's disheveled brown hair. His other grabbed three slices of bread and butter off a serving dish. "Mmm, I'm starving. Well, Junie?"

"I wanted to look up something, and there's no dictionary."

"What's the word?"

Junie made a face at her chowder. "It doesn't matter," she said. Then, "Dad, do heavy metals ever get magnetic?"

"You've got me," Sam said through a mouthful of bread. "Hey, Lyn, what do you think? Do heavy metals magnetize?"

"Iron does," Lyn said, frowning down at a journal article.

Sam shook his head in mock amazement. "The great mind does it again. Considering that iron just about defines magnetism—" He turned to Junie. "What kind of heavy metal did you mean, Junie?"

"I don't know. Just something that could pollute water, something a magnetometer might be able to find."

Lyn looked up. "Iron gets rusty in water. If you can think of orange water as polluted water—"

"Would I turn orange if I had a bath in it?" Kathy asked curiously.

"No, darling. Eat your clams."

"It's mean to eat clams," Kathy said.

Absently, Sam spooned some more chowder into his dish. "I'm no physicist, Junie, but I always thought magnetometers were used to measure changes in the earth's magnetic field. Due to sunspot activity, say. I never heard of them being used to measure water pollution."

Junie exchanged significant glances with Marty. "So if

someone was using one in water, what would they be looking for?"

"A shipwreck," Lynda said at once.

"Now, Lyn," Sam said.

"No, really. A lot of ships used to be made of iron. And before that, even the wooden ships had tons of iron cannon and shot. There's so much iron on ships, it can actually distort the local magnetic field. So with a magnetometer you could find even a silt-covered wreck that no one could see any other way. Stop looking at me like that, Sam Niven!"

"Did you actually see someone using a magnetometer underwater, Junie?" Sam asked curiously.

"Dr. Pembroke was. He—"

"He scared Marty," Kathy interrupted importantly. "Junie, too."

"He was wearing a wetsuit," Marty explained quickly. "All black and white. The fog made him seem . . ." Her voice trailed off.

"*Anyway,*" Junie said, with a quelling look at her sister, "Dr. Pembroke told us he was using the magnetometer to find magnetized heavy metals. Pollutants, he said."

Sam smiled. "So there's your answer."

"But you said you'd never heard of them being used for that."

"He's the pollution expert, Junie, not me. I can't keep up on my own field, let alone heavy metals." He shoveled three fast spoonfuls of chowder into his mouth and made a face. "Cold, damn it."

"Always happens when you start talking," Lyn said equably. "Oh, hi, Ray."

Pembroke had come over to their table. He put one foot up on the bench and grinned at Lyn, then winked impartially at the three girls. Marty noticed that his wineglass was in constant motion, the stem twirling between his index finger and thumb at exactly the rate needed to

59

make a continuous whirlpool in the red wine inside. Any faster, and it would have splashed out; slower or less steadily, and there would have been only little jerky waves.

Sam said, "We were just talking about you, Ray."

"I thought my ears were burning," Pembroke said cheerfully. "These girls of yours been telling you how they came on Bill and me doing mysterious things in the fog?"

"Junie and Kathy could turn a minister's sermon into a mysterious act," Lyn said, laughing. "I hope they weren't being pests."

"Pests!" Junie exclaimed indignantly.

"Regular gadflies, they were," Ray said, smiling at Junie, who shoved her chin out mutinously in response. "Wanted physics lessons on the spot—nice to see, actually, even though the tide was coming in, and fog everywhere."

"When did you start this heavy metal project?" Sam asked curiously. "I'd got the idea into my head that it was creosote you were interested in."

For one instant the wine in Pembroke's glass jerked. Then it was back swirling again as smoothly as before. "That's for places nearer to lumber mills. It's selenium I'm studying this summer. The runoff from irrigation in particular. People *will* irrigate deserts, and California deserts are time bombs where selenium is concerned."

"But selenium's not a heavy metal," Sam objected.

"Of course it isn't." Pembroke's smile seemed entirely natural, but again Marty noticed little jerky waves in his wineglass. "The thing is, it's usually found in combination with heavy metals, so we do the relatively easier search for them, and think about selenium afterward."

"Reasonable."

Marty frowned, thinking hard. At the Estero, Pembroke hadn't said a word about selenium. But maybe he thought they were too young to understand. And he'd answered Sam's questions fast enough. If Sam thought the answers were reasonable, who was she to let a wine glass make her wonder?

"How's your algae bloom study going, Sam?" Ray asked.

"Nothing provable yet, but there's more algae than I'd like at that kelp forest Ewan found off Double Point. Time will tell."

"You and Bill aren't going back to the *Leviathan* tonight, are you, Ray?" Lyn asked.

"Not in this fog."

"Where will you sleep?"

"Heather's found us a couple of sleeping bags. We'll stretch out here in the dining tent."

"Breakfast will wake you," Lyn said. "Why not stay in our tent, instead? We have loads of room."

"Thank you, Lyn, but we'll be off ourselves very early in the morning. Big funding meeting with the board in San Francisco." He made a face.

"What do they want?" Sam asked. "Not results already? The summer's barely begun. What are you going to tell them?"

Ray grinned. "Algae bloom off Double Point, didn't you say?"

"It only looked like that," Sam said hastily. "We haven't done the definitive tests. I wouldn't want—"

"Don't worry, Sam. I won't put you on the spot. It'll be something for the board to chew on, that's all."

He left them, then, joining Heather and Bill who were shaking out some sleeping bags. Dr. Anderson came into the dining tent a few moments later. He looked worried.

"What's the matter, Jonas?" Lyn asked, beckoning him over.

"You haven't seen that research assistant of mine, have you?" he asked, keeping his voice low.

"Nick, you mean? Why, no."

"Marty? Have you?" She shook her head. Half to himself, Dr. Anderson said, "He's probably just brooding over some computer problem, but with this fog..." Seeing Lyn's concerned face, he tried to smile. "*In loco parentis*, that's me. And you know how loco some parents get."

"I saw Nick in the rowboat earlier," Sam volunteered. "He was on his way out to the *Leviathan*. It was around four-thirty, before the fog really came on. He's bound to have gotten there all right."

Jonas Anderson chewed his lip. "Then I hope to hell he had the sense to stay there." His eyes shot nervously across the tent to Ray Pembroke's face.

"Couldn't you call the ship and find out?" Junie asked. "Heather has a two-way radio."

"Yes. Yes. I know." But his eyes were still on Pembroke. He didn't want to ask Heather to check up on Nick, Marty knew. And the reason clearly had something to do with Pembroke.

"He'd be furious with me for raising the alarm for nothing," Dr. Anderson said. "I'll give him ten more minutes."

"Sit down and have some chowder," Lyn said. "Time always passes more quickly if you're doing something."

Nick rested his arms on his oars. The water was oily, flattened by that palpable, squeezing weight of fog. There was no noise of surf to guide him. If he kept rowing toward what he thought was the shore or tried to return to the ship, he would probably just go in circles, or worse, end up out at sea. And the Point Reyes coast was one of the most dangerous in the world.

He strained his eyes into the fog. Nothing. Drops of water condensed on his eyelashes. What to do? What?

As he sat there, paralyzed with indecision, he heard something. It wasn't a noise, but a whole series of noises:

like a gong being drummed deep and soft. BONG, BONG, bong-bong-bong. It was almost something to feel rather than to hear. BONG, BONG, bong-bong. Louder now. BONG, BONG, bong-bong-bong. Loud! Loud! Nick clapped his hands to his ears, but nothing could keep out that deep, wild, thrumming song. It had become part of him, echoing and reechoing, making Nick vibrate with it, making him its instrument.

The water surged suddenly. The rowboat tossed like a cork. Terrified, Nick grabbed for the gunwales.

POOOH! It was a huge explosion of air, a smell like old fishnets and machine oil. Out of the fog came the profile of a head, unimaginably huge. Barnacled and baleened, the line of the mouth was almost as long as Nick was tall. It curved downward under a single intelligent eye. The eye regarded him expressionlessly, scarcely a boat length away.

For an endless moment they stared at each other, Nick and the whale. Then the whale sank slowly beneath the waves. A heartbeat later the boat surged forward. Nick grabbed again for the gunwales, but he was not really afraid. The boat moved again, another jerky movement forward. Slowly and carefully Nick leaned over the stern. The whale was there. He had known it would be. There was a second whale with it, less than a third the length of the first, though easily twice Nick's own size. A baby, obviously. Which meant the first whale was its mother.

The boat moved again, nudged by the whale's great head. Just enough thrust to push the boat through the water. Enough, and no more. No hint of what those gigantic muscles could actually do, had they been kept less carefully in check.

It was purposeful, then. Why? There might have been any reason, or none: an accident, repeated over and over; a game Nick didn't understand; some kind of alien teaching between the mother and her calf. But it was none of these things. Nick knew it without knowing how he knew. He knew what was really happening.

Slowly, almost gently, the whale was pushing him to shore.

CHAPTER SIX

"LOOK AT KATHY," LYN SAID. "ASLEEP ON her feet."

"I'm not," Kathy said, and yawned hugely.

"How anybody's going to sleep tonight, I don't know." Anxiously Lyn consulted her watch.

Nick still wasn't back. Dr. Anderson had waited as long as he could to tell Heather and Pembroke, and was angry with himself afterward, when they radioed the ship and learned that Nick had started back for shore in the fog more than an hour before. Now Paul Wilson and Pembroke were setting up two fog flares, one behind the other, to help Nick find his way in. There was, as Pembroke said, very little else anyone could do, in this fog.

Everyone talked worriedly about the danger Nick was in, alone in a small boat, lost in the fog on that bay whose boundaries were the graveyard of countless ships. People talked about rock stacks and wave action, about great white sharks and hypothermia. It all seemed very unreal to Marty. She knew no one was exaggerating the threat, but somehow she couldn't link it to Nick. Something inside her, stubborn and illogical, was absolutely certain that Nick had come to no harm. He would be back in camp soon. Whatever reason he had for being late, it wasn't because he was in trouble.

Not that kind of trouble, anyway.

She shifted uneasily in her chair. Despite her certainty about Nick's safety, she couldn't shake the feeling that something important, even dangerous, had started out

65

there in the fog today. Or maybe earlier? She couldn't be sure. Something had begun, some course of events with its own life; but deciding when it had started was as hard as deciding when a sound was loud enough to hear.

She got to her feet. "I'll get Kathy ready for bed," she said to Lyn.

She didn't want to be there when Nick got back. People would be angry at him. They would demand to know why he had left the *Leviathan* in the fog. They would act as if what he'd done was a stupid, thoughtless thing. They would never imagine that he had had a reason. She thought of the fury and hate in his eyes, talking about Drake and that boy John Doughty. She had known then that it wasn't just the *Golden Hind* he was angry about. Whether he told anybody or not, Nick had had a reason.

The calf had nursed hardly at all, and the mother's body ached from too much milk. It was too soon for the calf to be completely weaned. She tried, wearily, to remember the last time she had seen hard-backed foods in its mouth. Not long, she thought. Not very long.

She wished they could leave this place. But there were songs that, once begun, had to be sung through to their ends. Softly, hypnotically, she moved her flukes up and down in the water, sending cool ripples against the calf's unbarnacled body. Mischievously, it blew bubbles back at her. Her heart lightened. It would be all right.

She thought again of that two-legged male today, lost in his log in the water-thick air. How bitterly his mind had sung, like vapor spreading out from sea ice, penetrating and cold. His was a song the People had heard before. "Nothing to be done. A man kills your brother, and nothing to be done."

She pondered the meaning. *Man* was clear: It was what

they called themselves, as the People were the People. *Brother* was harder: a loved one, perhaps a podmate? One of its own kind, certainly. "A man kills your brother." Among the People, only the orca killed its own kind.

Two singers, one song. The one today adrift in his tiny log, thinking of the man who had killed his podmate; the other cast out long ago from a much bigger log by the man who had killed *his* podmate.

She opened her mind to the People's whole memory, and the scene flooded in. That long-ago singer tossed into the water, his poor unblubbered body shuddering with cold, those inefficient blowholes sucking in water instead of air. The People hearing his song, and coming. Looking upon him curiously; comparing what he sang to things they, too, knew; turning thoughtful eyes up to that log where a man stood, still and hot, staring down. The People knew what it was to face an orca. Pitying the one in the water, they supported him so that his blowholes were free to breathe, keeping him warm with the press of their bodies, bringing him food-creatures when he would have died from want of them. Suns rose and fell, and in the end, the man in the log lifted the singer again, and did not kill him.

And that, too, was the orca's way, unpredictable and capable, dark and light together, singing its own rich dissonance.

Wooden logs, sticks splashing into the water, man killing man. In the face of an orca, the People always tried to save what was being attacked. Now or then, then or now? It did not matter. When a song is marked for repetition, can the singer ignore it?

Unbidden, the calf had heard the mother's thoughts. Rubbing its head against hers, it said, *Pushing a man's log to land is not the same as giving that man air or food.*

Not all refrains repeat exactly, calfling.

67

Then how do you know it was a refrain? Did the Song repeat on its own, or did you choose to repeat it?

The mother rose twice to breathe, unable to reply. At last she said, *Calves in trouble are everywhere, even among the two-legged ones. Could any mother among the People have turned away?*

Kathy was sleeping, curled up in the tent. Outside in the foggy night, Marty was making the rounds of the window flaps, tying them back just enough to allow in a little air without making the tent too damp. She had heard the uproar when Nick came back, and was glad he was safe, without being surprised. He would be eating now, eyes on his plate, while Dr. Anderson would be trying not to say whatever it was that he knew about Nick hurrying away from the *Leviathan*. Everybody else would be pretending not to watch. Poor Nick. She was glad she wasn't there.

The Coleman lamp she carried cast a white circle of light onto the ground beside her. She moved slowly from one window to the next, her mind flitting from Nick to magnetometers and shipwrecks to that odd, powerful sense of something starting, events unrolling like a carpet, catching everything in its path. Pembroke, coming out of the fog and smiling his odd, crooked smile; Nick, with his hatred of a man who four hundred years ago could eat a hearty meal and then chop off a friend's head. Nick, who hated a great deal more than that.

"Marty?" It was a deep voice, oddly urgent.

She almost dropped the lamp. "Who is it?" she got out, peering into the fog.

"Just me." Nick came into the light. For a minute he only stood there. He didn't seem to know what to do with his hands. One moment they were in his pockets.

Then they were out tugging at his hair or fiddling with his watch. Then they were back in his pockets again. "I thought you might like some help."

His awkwardness made her less nervous. "I'm just done. But thanks."

"Some company, then?"

But it was Nick, she thought, who wanted company. His face was very pale and strained. She said, "Were people really mad at you?"

"A bit. I guess it was pretty dumb, rowing back in that fog. I deserved getting yelled at."

"By Dr. Pembroke?" Marty didn't know why she asked that, only that it had something to do with the way Jonas Anderson hadn't wanted to tell Pembroke that Nick was missing.

Nick made a face. "Not him. It was Dr. Anderson who was mad."

"That was only because he was worried about you." She looked at him. "Something did happen out there in the fog, didn't it?"

"You might say so," he muttered, and laughed, shortly. "I—God, Marty, you're going to think I'm crazy. I mean, miracles don't happen anymore, do they? You get lost, that's it, you're lost. A great big whale doesn't come out of the fog with her baby and push your rowboat to shore."

"A whale?" She blinked at him. "Nick, you didn't see one? Here? Oh, Nick, you did!"

In her gladness she moved a step closer to him. Her long hair swept forward, just brushing his hand. He closed his fingers around a strand of it. She was sure he didn't know he was doing it. People grabbed on to things. He didn't mean anything by it. But it felt strange, standing there, linked to him this way, unable to move without making the link more obvious. "How—I mean, why do you think the whale—?" His fingers moved in her hair. She broke off, scarlet faced.

"I've figured it all out since then," he said. "The tide was going out, but big deal, it would probably only have taken me back to the *Leviathan*. Even if it hadn't, tides are slow. As long as I didn't row, I probably wouldn't have ended up out to sea before the fog lifted. The worst that would have happened would have been drifting into a rock. Even that's no problem when there's no surf, like today. There was nothing for me to worry about."

He was speaking faster and faster, not waiting for her to answer. If it hadn't been for his fingers in her hair, she would have thought he didn't even know that she was there.

"I could have yelled out to the *Leviathan*. Stinking ship, so white, couldn't see it in the fog. White, that's a joke, with Richard's guts all over its insides! We didn't want him to go with Pembroke, but we were never scared for him. And I wasn't scared today. Stupid whale, I didn't need it! Why didn't it leave me alone?"

She didn't move. She didn't dare move. He talked on and on, holding her hair and telling her things about his brother who had died, about the man he blamed for it, about the father who had gotten him this job, and why. She listened, and could say nothing; she had never in her life felt so inadequate. He talked for a long time, and then, for another long time, he didn't talk. But always he held her hair, now loose, now tight, now softly stroking, finger and thumb running up and down the shaft, gentle.

And then, somehow, he was gone, leaving her quiet in the lamplight, her hand on the hair he had touched.

Why had he told her all that stuff?

In his sleeping bag Nick lay sleepless, his eyes wide open. Marty's tent was only a short distance away. Nick alternated between wishing it were farther and being angry with himself for wanting the exact opposite. How *could* he have talked to her so much? All his deciding to stay anonymous this summer, to get through this job without telling anyone about his connection to Richard or Pembroke, and then the first chance he got he dropped it all in Marty's lap!

"I'll be confiding to Pembroke next," Nick muttered.

Pembroke. Bitterness flooded Nick again, remembering how nice the man had been to him tonight. That sympathetic look he'd given Nick when Dr. Anderson had started his lecture about water safety, the way he'd gripped Nick's shoulder and steered him to a bowl of hot chowder when the lecture was over. Okay. Okay! So Pembroke could be decent. No news there. Richard wouldn't have been taken in by an ordinary slime ball.

In his tent, staring wide eyed into the darkness, Nick could see and hear nothing at all. Night was a black fog, surrounding him with its profound, insubstantial walls. He might have been the only person in the whole of Point Reyes.

It was the way he liked it, he told himself. On his own, relying on nobody, in control.

So why had he told Marty what he had?

It was because of the whale, obviously. Coming out of the fog like that, its song echoing inside of him, as if it were his song, too. Pushing him to shore, whether he needed it or not! Anybody would have wanted to talk about it.

Then why hadn't he told Dr. Duguay, who actually studied whales? Or Dr. Anderson, who shared a tent with him, and who would have been interested, even if it wasn't his field of research? Why Marty, of all people?

And why tell her about all that other stuff, afterward, the stuff that had nothing to do with the whale?

If she had said just one thing, he would have stopped. But she hadn't. She had just stood there and listened and he hadn't been able to dam the flood of words pouring out of him. Had she minded? Had she noticed him holding on to her hair? Like that six-year-old kid she baby-sat! God!

He would stay right away from her from now on. He would do his job and forget her.

And the whales? His fingers clenched. He would forget them, too.

There was no sunshine the next day, or the next. Pockets of fog lay like misty lakes in the hollows. There was not enough wind to dry the tents, and the moisture that dripped from the nylon tent flies made puddles in the tough yellow grass. In camp, people wore raincoats and boots and thick clothing underneath to keep out the penetrating damp. Those few scientists who were able to relocate their studies inland came back sunburned and cheerful and talking about local variations in the weather. But for the majority, whose studies were focused either on the shore or right out on the water, the conditions were miserable: clear enough, or only just, to do the work, but still so foggy and cold that everything took twice the effort. "Summer in California," someone grumbled at supper one night. "Give me a Vancouver winter any day."

Marty and the girls spent most of Wednesday biking to Chimney Rock. It was too far for Kathy, so Marty took the little girl on the back of her own bike. They walked the last mile in a fog that thickened the closer they got to the edge of the sea. Everyone had said the view would be spectacular, but when they got to the overlook all they saw was mist. It was a lonely feeling, peering out into emptiness, hearing the incessant bark of invisible sea lions and the long swoosh of ocean swell breaking unseen on the cliffs below. At the other end of the point a foghorn mooed its dreary two-tone warning. There was nowhere dry to sit. They ate their picnic lunch standing up and started back right away. Kathy and Junie argued almost the whole way home.

On Thursday the weather was no better. Junie refused flatly to leave the camp. Marty couldn't leave her alone, so she and Kathy stayed, too, playing board games while Junie read. It was a dismal day. At lunch they ate in the dining tent with Ann Duguay and her graduate student, Glenna, listening to true stories about some dolphins they had studied. Marty enjoyed it until Nick came in. He didn't look at her, just made himself a sandwich and went out again, back to his tent to work. Since the night he had told her about his brother, he had shown very plainly that he didn't want to have anything to do with her.

She was sure she knew why. That night, he had needed somebody to talk to. Anybody would have done, but it had happened to be her. And she hadn't helped. She hadn't been able to say one single thing to take away his anger and his despair. She hadn't, she remembered miserably, been able to say anything at all. She had just stood there. He probably thought she was the stupidest person alive.

On Saturday the weather cleared. Boots and coats were shoved into storage, and people who had barely nodded to one another in the last few days chatted and joked at breakfast like old friends. Paul Wilson had set up a lot of chairs outside the dining tent, and almost everybody was eating outside. The sky was a warm, clear blue. For the first time in three days it felt like summer.

"What a day for Golden Gate Park!" Sam said, stretching out his long legs in the sunshine.

Beside him, Lynda had her eyes half closed, both hands cupped around her coffee mug. Kathy was seeing how much of her bacon bun she could fit into her mouth at once. Now and then, seeing someone watching her, she grinned, revoltingly. Junie was in the tent, deciding what to take to San Francisco for the day. In a way, Marty wished she were going with them, though Sam and Lynda were right about her needing time off from the kids.

Yesterday she had been so worn out from refereeing three days of their bickering that she had gone to bed right after supper. She hadn't slept very well, though. She had kept waking in a sweat, gasping for air and not knowing what she had dreamed or why it had made her so afraid.

She was very aware of Nick standing at the lookout by the barrier in his usual isolation. Today he was going to Tomales Point to learn how to take measurements for Dr. Anderson's study. Marty had heard Dr. Anderson mention it while offering a lift to Art Dunn, the physicist whose small tent stood beside his own. Art usually bicycled out to his water-flow studies, but today Glenna Hoyt was going with him, and she didn't like bike riding. Marty could see Glenna, lipsticked and pretty, standing a little too close to Art at the serving table. Art looked almost as uncomfortable as that first night, when he had talked to her only about fluid dynamics.

Paul Wilson was at the top of the path, pushing the wagonlike provisions cart they used to transport supplies and water to and from the camp. The administrative officer, Heather Kent, was with him. "Tacos tonight," she called to them. "I know it's the first of July, but we did serve Canadian bacon this morning!"

Marty remembered with surprise that it was Canada Day. At home, everybody would be partying.

"Last call for Tomales Point," Dr. Anderson said, getting up from his chair.

Art and Glenna gathered their things together and followed him down the path. Nick came and picked up his knapsack from where he'd dropped it, near where Marty sat beside Sam and Lynda. He glanced at Marty, almost said something, then checked himself, gave a wry shrug, and headed after the others. It was the closest he'd come to speaking to her in three days.

Junie came out of the tent, her arms full of books. "I

can't decide which of these to take," she said, "so I'm bringing them all."

"We're only going for one day," Lyn said, yawning.

Kathy eyed the books thoughtfully, spat out her bun, and got up. "Race you to the van, Junie!" She was off.

"She'll say she won," Junie said huffily, "and I'm not even racing. Bye, Marty. Use my bird book if you want to. *Kathy!*"

Sam shoved back his chair. "Come on, Lyn. You're on discipline duty today. I'm just the driver, thank heavens."

They were gone.

CHAPTER SEVEN

VERY SLOWLY, MARTY FINISHED HER COF-
fee. She put her mug with the other dirty
dishes, then collected and scraped some plates
other people had forgotten. She took her sleeping bag out of her tent and laid it in the sun. She got a
broom and swept up the dried mud she had tracked into
her tent yesterday. She went into the Nivens' big tent,
took all four of their sleeping bags outside, and spread
them beside her own. Finally she allowed herself to look
at her watch. Only ten-thirty. It was going to be a long
day.

Aimlessly, she wandered through the deserted camp.
Someone had put a sign up outside the dining tent. NO
TRESPASSING, the sign said. SCIENTIFIC RESEARCH IN
PROGRESS. DO NOT DISTURB SITE. In the crowded parking
lot, a few curious tourists were already making a beeline
for the tarmac trail leading up to the camp. Marty hurried
back to her tent and zipped the doorway to make it
less inviting to visitors, then went back to the railed-off
lookout. The tourists joined her. "Hi," they said. "Great
view, huh?"

She smiled and nodded and leaned her chin against the
railing, staring out over the water. After a while the tourists went away, but she stayed on. A warm wind was
blowing, and the water was a calm, glittering blue. Out
on Drake's Bay the *Leviathan* lay at anchor, showing no
sign of life. The rubber dinghy that usually hung on its

davit was gone. Was Ray Pembroke out there with his magnetometer again, he and that diver called Bill?

Not very far offshore, a puff of white smoke caught her eye. There was no ship there; nothing to cause that smoke. And it couldn't be a cloud, not that close to the water. It lingered for a moment, then dissipated. Like someone's breath on a frosty day, Marty thought. She watched carefully. There! Again! And was that a second puff beside the first?

Without knowing how she got there, she found herself on the beach. It was crowded with people playing Frisbee and drinking from cans. She hurried past them, splashing through the little stream that bisected the beach, then jogging across the pale sand to the very edge of the sea. There she waited, waves lapping her wet sneakers, her gaze darting here and there across the water. Nothing. She began to walk southeast along the shoreline, keeping her eyes on the water. She walked a long time. The sunbathers were left behind, and there were fewer hikers. She didn't notice. She was on the same beach she and Junie and Kathy had walked on Tuesday when the fog had rolled in. She hadn't seen much of it then, and she saw no more today. She had eyes only for the water.

Some distance along, the breaks began to get bigger. She walked a little farther, then stopped, waiting. Time passed; she didn't know how long. Suddenly, in the surf right in front of her there came a blinding glint of sunlight, sprays of water droplets turning the sky to a prism. The dazzle turned off, sudden as a switch. Marty's breath caught in her throat. Something wet and large had broken the surface. It was big, impossibly big, like a tanker truck turned on end, only alive. Torpedo shaped and flippered, it arched its powerful, overwhelming life out of the water, pleated throat angling into the sky, half-closed eyes not looking at Marty, yet knowing that she was there.

Breathe, calfling. Air is life. Breathe.

Marty's breath shuddered out and in. Water fountained up, an enormous splash. When she could see again, there were two ridged outlines, one longer than the other, on the surface of the water. A moment later they were gone. She stared and stared, but she had lost them. Mother and baby both were gone.

It was so quiet in the campsite that she could hear Paul Wilson whistling inside the dining tent. She got her knapsack from her tent, filled her thermos with water at the spigoted cask that Sam had fixed up outside, and left again, all without seeing a soul.

The whale had talked to her. She had heard it. It had told her to breathe. It had called her "Calfling."

She climbed the steep path behind the Visitors' Center. Up on the bluffs she shaded her eyes, scanning the bay for pale spouts. Nothing. Purposefully, she began hiking along the coastal bluffs. Every few minutes she stopped and swept her gaze around the bay. If the whales had gone farther out, she had a better chance up here of seeing their spouts. But there might have been no whales in the entire world, for all she saw of them. When she came to the two-lane track, she hesitated. The whales weren't going to show themselves. Squinting and staring into the bright blue water was useless. It was better not to be able to see the water at all. She turned, shoulders shoved back, and marched along the track in the opposite direction from the one she and the girls had taken the other day. Inland, away from the bay.

She had heard a whale speak. It had spoken to her, to Marty Griffiths, who could barely pass biology. And now a whale had spoken to her. To her!

The farther from the water she got, the more unsure she became. Whales didn't speak to humans. In school Marty had heard a record of whale sounds, a strange and unearthly pattern of creaking high pitches alternating in odd rhythms with long, low vibrations that made her body ache. Those sounds hadn't been remotely close to words; but it was words, English words, that Marty had heard the whale say.

The whale hadn't even opened its mouth, she reminded herself. She had been watching it the whole time, and the whale's mouth had never moved.

But a moment later the calf had joined its mother. Could the mother have called it in her mind to come to the surface to breathe, and had Marty somehow tuned in to that communication and thought the whale was speaking to her? But then how had she understood it?

The more she thought about it, the more certain it seemed that she had only imagined that deep, gentle voice in her mind.

Sick with disappointment, she stopped short, staring unseeingly at a milk thistle her own height, replaying the scene in her mind. The aching joy of it washed over her again. The glinting sunlight. Bluish gray body in a dazzle of spray. Eyes half shut, like Lynda at breakfast, face raised to the summer sky while Kathy quietly misbehaved beside her. Warmth and caring in her mind, luxuriation, half-amused understanding as if the whale were saying, *I'm not something you need to hold your breath about! Breathe, silly child, breathe!*

She shook her hair back off her face and walked on. It had happened. She hadn't made it up. The whale had spoken. She knew now how Nick had felt, that time in the fog when the whale had pushed him ashore. It was all so impossible, and yet it had happened.

Dr. Anderson brought Nick and the others back early from Tomales Point. At lunch Glenna had reminded them that it was Canada Day. Art had grumbled about there being just two months left till the fall term, but Dr. Anderson had laughed. "It's Saturday, Art, *and* it's a holiday. You've got time to raise a glass for your country. Get him back to the car at three, Glenna. And you, Nick, keep an eye on your watch."

There were quite a few people in the camp for the middle of an afternoon. In spite of himself, Nick scanned the campsite for Marty. He didn't know whether to be relieved or disappointed when he couldn't find her. She had looked so isolated and quiet, sitting there among that noisy Niven family this morning, that he had almost forgotten his vow and spoken to her. It was that same silence of hers that had gotten him into trouble the other night, making him tell her things. He remembered the silky, scented length of her hair wound about his palm, the way he couldn't make himself let go, words flowing out of him into the white circle of lamplight. And Marty, standing there so still. Listening, absorbing, no part of her intruding, dark eyes shining, lips parted, head tilted, almost not breathing rather than make a movement that would distract him from what he had to say.

Had to say. Angrily, Nick shook his head. There was nothing he had to say to other people, nothing he couldn't handle by himself. He made himself join the crowd of people in front of the dining tent.

"You're Canadian, Nick, so the beer's on us," Paul said, offering him a can, "but we'll expect you to return the favor on the Fourth of July."

Nick took the can. Some people thought seventeen was too young for beer. He drank deeply. It tasted bitter, so he drank some more. A little while later, when he had finished the first can, someone handed him another. He drank that too.

Heather Kent came over to him. "Nice to see people loosen up," she said, smiling. "You, for instance. First time I've seen you have any fun since you arrived." Her body was all curves and bulges, not at all like Marty's.

He smiled up at her, as widely as he could manage. "Great party. Great."

She sat down beside him. He couldn't think of one thing to say. She told him everything she had done that day, starting and ending with shopping. He listened.

There was still no sign of Marty.

At four-thirty, he got abruptly to his feet and left Heather looking puzzled. He went over to Paul Wilson, who had been in camp most of the day. "You see Marty today?" he demanded abruptly.

"Let me think," Paul said, opening a can. It seemed to take forever. "Seems to me, I did. Now when—? Oh, yeah, it was while I was taking out the coffee urn for lunch. She was up on the bluffs behind the Visitors' Center. Hiking along the bay, it looked like."

By the time Nick had climbed to the top of the cliff behind the center, he had gotten it all straight in his head. Marty was just a kid, and alone. Sam and Lynda weren't here today to look after her. She had been gone for hours, and could have gotten into all kinds of trouble in a wilderness like Point Reyes. It was up to him, since no one else had noticed, to try to find her.

There was no sign of her on the treeless uplands. But if she was down in one of those narrow sea-level valleys that alternated with the bluffs, he wouldn't be able to see her from where he stood. She wasn't in the first dip he came to, but there was a two-pronged lake there, and a dirt track circling it. He followed the track as far as the foot of the next cliff, where he left the track and began to climb again. He wasn't moving as fast as before. Marty might look like a kid, but she was in charge of two others a lot younger than herself. For five whole days she had taken them wherever they wanted to go and not gotten into any trouble. Why would she suddenly have problems today?

Halfway up the cliff he slowed down even more. Maybe

she wouldn't like him coming out after her like this. Would she think it was chauvinistic? And since when had he played at being Sir Galahad, anyway?

I'll go back, he thought.

But he was almost at the top; he might as well climb the rest of the way. And when he got there, he would walk a bit farther, just enough to make the climb worthwhile. He wouldn't be looking for Marty, just getting a bit of fresh air to clear his head.

He couldn't think of a time when it had needed clearing more.

Marty didn't walk very far inland. Even with her back to the sea, even far enough away from it that she could neither hear it nor smell it, she simply couldn't stop herself turning around every few minutes, straining to catch a glimpse of the watery horizon. When the dirt track she was on led to a farmer's fence, she hopped over and cut across the pasture to the highway, then followed it back down to the parking lot at Drake's Bay. There was no point avoiding something if you couldn't stop thinking about it.

Near the Visitors' Center she hesitated. It was late in the afternoon, and she hadn't had any lunch, but the idea of going back to camp didn't appeal to her. It would be full of Coleman smells and clattering pots and chattering, noisy people. The beach would be full of people, too, but at least there she wouldn't have to make conversation. She went a new way down to the beach, not crossing the little stream that angled across it, but instead scrambling alongside it over rocks and sandy shelves until it turned toward the bay at the foot of the cliffs. There was a single small rowboat in the inlet there, with a sign in it. PRIVATE PROPERTY OF THE CONSERVOCEAN FOUNDATION, it said. UNAUTHORIZED USE FORBIDDEN. Someone had forgotten to take out the oars.

The tide was going out. Even the shallowest depressions held seawater, and rock formations that hadn't been there before stood up out of the sand. Suddenly tired, Marty plodded over to one that was draped with seaweed, wet sand sucking insistently at her feet and filling her footprints with water. She knelt by the tide pool in the rock. It was a small world of sea lettuce and barnacles, snails and busily swimming sea slugs. She watched it for a long time, so still that a guillemot landed right beside her and paddled its bright red feet in the water. As it gobbled its panicking prey, Marty told herself that it had to eat. But after a minute she waved her arms at the bird, trying to scare it off. The guillemot, not much bigger than her hand, defied her with shrill, mouselike squeaks before giving up and flying away. Close by, two tiny hermit crabs warred over a piece of crushed mussel. Gulls swooped and screamed. Everywhere, unavoidable, was the stink of dead fish, thrown up by the tide.

Living in Vancouver all her life, Marty was no stranger to the smells and sounds and the deadly little battles that took place on beaches. But she had rarely noticed them before today, and never disliked them. Yet now this intertidal beach made her feel a little sick. She stared longingly out at the clean, cold swell of the deeper bay. If only the whales would show themselves again!

Logically, she knew that they might be far away by now, that their visit to Nick on Tuesday and to her today might be nothing more than chance, that they might have taken it into their heads to leave Point Reyes this morning and never come back. But she didn't believe it. Those two whales, mother and baby, were out in the bay right this minute. They couldn't come close to land now that the tide was going out, and she couldn't see their spouts because of the low fluff of cloud on the horizon, but they were out there somewhere. If only she could get farther

83

out on the water herself, she might see them. The mother might even talk to her again.

Marty was a good swimmer, but the deeper bay was too icy to swim in without a wet suit. There were plenty of wet suits in the camp; probably half the scientists had them. But Marty couldn't borrow one without people asking why she wanted it. If she told them the truth, the scientists would try to study the whales; they would tag them so that their instruments would always know where the whales were; the mother and baby would never again be free of scientific scrutiny. She couldn't do that to them.

Marty stood with her head bowed, thinking about the rowboat she had seen in the cove. PROPERTY OF THE CONSERVOCEAN FOUNDATION. But it was late in the day. Any scientist who might have needed the boat would have taken it long ago. And she was part of the foundation, in a way. She was sure no one would mind if she borrowed it.

Nick had seen the whales from a rowboat. They had come right up to him, and the mother had laid her great head against the boat and pushed.

She turned away from the shore, clambering the rocks so swiftly she almost fell into the little inlet. She bent over the bow of the rowboat, a hand on each gunwale. The wood felt warm. The sea smell rose from it, weedy, like olives and old socks. Experimentally, she gave the boat a little push. It moved. She pushed again. With a grate and a hiss the boat slid over the pebbles into the stream. She jerked it around so that it faced the bay. Now it pushed easily. She imagined the oars in her hands, dipping and pulling, the boat obeying her, taking her where she wanted to go.

And the boat was out in the bay, and she was in the boat, and the oars were in her hands, and she was rowing.

CHAPTER EIGHT

 NOW THAT HE HAD DECIDED TO STOP looking for Marty, Nick tried to enjoy his walk. He looked at the views, changing with every minute; he sniffed the faint, salty breeze; he identified fading wildflowers among the sere summer grasses; he even counted varieties of birds. But whenever he tried to concentrate, images flashed against the back of his eyes: burned-sugar hair sweeping around a dancer's body; a whale's eye, big enough to drown in; Richard, slinging his pack onto the bus that would take him to join Pembroke, smart and in charge and waving good-bye.

All the blood's gone, Richard, and you don't even know. They cleaned it up, it didn't last, they fixed the ship but they couldn't fix you. You're gone, you're a stone with writing on it, and Mom cries and Dad cries, and they want me to, too, but why should I, when it was you who decided to go?

Going, always going, homework in the kitchen and cookies and ordinary life given up for wilderness campfires and the howling of wolves and Ban the Bomb demonstrations. Asking for trouble, and getting it, and coming out on top, surviving.

And always coming back, until now.

Nick crouched by a tiny five-rayed flower, but didn't see it. He saw only two sets of blue-jeaned legs stretched out side by side in a campfire silence, two paddles dipping into still waters in the breath-holding mistiness of twilit lakes, bacon frying and moonrise over creamy canvas and a small boy crying from a nightmare and a bigger one gathering him, sleeping bag and all, into his arms.

I should never have come to Point Reyes, Nick thought, despairing. I had it all figured out till I came here.

On land nothing was ever this clear. On land the edges of things were softer, even the light blurred with dust. But out on the water there was so much clarity it almost hurt Marty's eyes. Brightness surrounded her: seawater smashing into rocks in a glittering spray; rounded swells with white, curling tongues; soaring gulls outlined feather by feather against a sky much bluer than it had seemed from the shore. The wind was stronger, too. Its sharp tang sat on Marty's tongue.

She was nearing Chimney Rock. Ahead of her loomed seastacks, the stubborn granite remains of a bigger, long-drowned Point Reyes. The stacks were patchworks of odd-shaped stones, jutting here, receding there, some of the ridges weedy and damp, others white with bird drop-pings. Cormorants roosted on each one. A few rubber-necked at Marty as she shipped her oars, but the rest didn't bother. At the foot of the cliffs a little way off, a pair of sea lions yelped at each other. It was their usual, incessant bark, a conversation, unalarmed. Marty's pres-ence disturbed them no more than it did the cormorants.

For a long time she only sat in the boat with her chin in her hand. Now and then, when she noticed the currents taking her too near a rock, she took up the oars and maneuvered the little boat back to its former position. She had rowed to this place without any reason to believe that the whales would be here. Now, with the same rea-sonless certainty, she waited for them to come.

Half drowsing in the warm sun, she let the time pass. The sun-dazzled water was blinding. She made her eyes into slits, then closed them altogether. Behind her eyelids her blood pounded, turning the brightness she had shut

86

out into a sea of red. She swam in it, down, down, red fading out, then orange, warm colors disappearing one by one, down to a place of indigo and violet, then deeper still, to the cold, crushing darkness at the bottom of the world.

There was no food there, only dead things, silty. Even the fish—the water-breathers—were few, ball eyed and bony, flicking their internal lights on and off to mesmerize what prey they could find. Down there, the lungs flattened and eye muscles twisted to knots in the skull, and the inner ear vibrated endlessly to the tearing and chewing of the world above, the gurgles of digestion, the rippling of gills, and the grating of bones sliding one against the next. Rising, then, blood throbbing purple behind changing eyes, up and up with pupils diminishing, shooting through thermoclines, color returning and eye muscles relaxing and lenses changing shape to accommodate the light and the air. Eyelids squinting into vision.

Marty's head jerked. She was sprawled out along the bottom boards, her neck stiff from being pillowed on her arm. Over the gunwale she could see the shoreline, white cliffs very near. There was a strange, oily taste in her mouth, and she was disturbingly aware of the air hissing through her nostrils. She sat up, carefully because her hair had caught in the oarlock. She had to work to free it, and was startled how cold and wet it felt. Her clothes were soaked through.

She blinked around her. The sky was a pale rose-gray, clouds heaped like dust balls on the horizon. Chimney Rock was gloomy in the distance, the wide Drake's Bay beach just off her bow. How had she drifted so far without noticing? She must have been asleep for a long time, so long that the tide had turned and taken her inshore, and the spray had wet her to the skin.

And the whales? Memory flashed at her: a roman candle flare of something swimming by her eyes. It was gone before she could identify it, but the feeling remained, an elusive happiness. Had she dreamed it, or had something really happened?

Suddenly, she was hungry. She looked at her watch and stifled a yelp. She had missed dinner. If she didn't hurry, she wouldn't be back before Sam and Lynda and the girls got home from San Francisco. She swiveled the oars over the sides and dug in deeply, remembering how angry people had been with Nick, coming back so late that night in the fog. He, at least, had had a reason to be out in the rowboat. She had taken this one without asking.

As long as she got back before the Nivens, everything would be all right. No one else would notice she wasn't there.

She set her jaw against the thought, and rowed on.

There was no trail along the edge of the bluffs, but Nick went that way, anyway. Pebbles skittered down the precipitous drop as he walked. He knew he was disturbing the precarious balance of the clifftop, but he didn't care. Whatever harm he did would be done by the ocean in the end, anyway. It was only a matter of time.

After about twenty minutes he came to a temporary end of the bluffs. In front of him was a drowned valley, the water rimmed with mud flats and sand dunes. It was separated from Drake's Bay only by a narrow, sandy ridge, and even that extended just two-thirds of the way across the valley. The rest was open water, a channel linking the still waters of the valley with the lines of surf out in the bay. Beyond that channel the bluffs continued, but Nick could go no farther without turning inland.

Nick knew where he was. This water-filled valley was too big to be anything but Drake's Estero, Sir Francis Drake's safe harbor that had been mentioned in Dr. Anderson's book. In this natural landscape devoid of modern constructions, it was easy to picture the *Golden*

Hind at anchor, waiting for the tide to go down so that the carpenters could get to work on her bottom boards, tar already boiling in pots on the shore and the men collecting wood from the forests that had covered the hills then, the boatswain whistling his orders, the gentlemen hunting with their harquebuses the little animals they called conies. Might John Doughty have stood once in this very spot and looked down, seeing the *Golden Hind* being worked on? Nick shook his head. John would have been down there with the others. If anybody had had to work his guts out, it would have been him.

While Nick was watching, a small, motorized rubber dinghy came into view on the bay. It was keeping very close to the surf line and heading slowly in the direction of the channel that went into the Estero. Now that it was no longer hidden by the bluffs, Nick realized he had been listening to its motor's soft growl for some time. Curiously, he watched it. It looked familiar: white, with red markings. He frowned. The *Leviathan* had a rubber dinghy that color.

There was only one man in the boat, but a towline was stretched taut behind it, angling down into the water. When the boat got to a point just past the entrance to the Estero, a float bobbed to the surface some distance behind it. It was a small red pennant easily visible from above, though from water level, with wave action to contend with, it would be harder to see. But the man in the boat must have been very alert, because almost at once the motor cut out. As the boat lost headway, the man scribbled something on a clipboard, and at the same moment a sleek black head appeared beside the pennant. For a moment Nick wondered if it was a seal, but then a black-clad arm came out of the water near the head and waved to the man in the boat, who cupped his hands around his mouth and yelled, "What'd you find, Ray?"

Ray. And that dinghy so much like the one from the

Leviathan. And Dr. Anderson saying that Pembroke spent most of his time out testing for chemicals along the coast. Nick squinted into the glittering water, but the scuba diver's face was a white, featureless blob. Pembroke's? It was impossible to tell.

"Pistol, hardly even corroded," the diver shouted back. "Late sixteenth century, and if it isn't English, I'll eat it!"

It didn't sound like Pembroke's ordinary speaking voice, but then the man was yelling. Nick dropped to the ground, wriggling out to the edge of the bluff where he could see without being seen.

"The second Drake artifact in this area in a week," exulted the man in the dinghy. "That frigate's simply got to be nearby. I'll bet we've sailed over it a dozen times!"

"If we have, the magnetometer doesn't show it. I'm starting to think—"

A raven rose from the clifftop, croaking loudly. When Nick could hear again, the man in the water was saying, "—never know who might be listening." His white blob of a face twisted from side to side as he scanned the shoreline.

Nick pressed his forehead against the ground. While he was like this, unable to see, the dinghy's motor started again. He waited a minute, then carefully raised his head. The boat was making a wide circle through the waves, turning back toward the man in the water. Nick watched as the driver cut the motor and helped Pembroke—if it was Pembroke—into the dinghy. Another roar, brief this time, and the boat again stopped, only a little away from the little red pennant in the waves. The man in the wet suit did something with what might have been a compass. The boat moved again, and again it stopped while the wetsuited man fiddled. This happened two more times. Then, finally, the dinghy roared back to where the pennant still floated. A moment later, the boat was off again, heading up the coast in the direction it had first appeared. The pennant was gone.

Nick lay still, thinking hard. An ancient English pistol, the second artifact the men had found that week. You don't find two artifacts in a week by accident. Anyway, they'd as good as said they were hunting for the wreck of some frigate. But Pembroke was a chemical oceanographer and fund-raiser; what possible reason could he have to be wreck hunting?

Unless the funds he was raising were shipwrecked treasure?

He shook his head angrily. All this from a first name and a dinghy that looked like one on the *Leviathan*! "Face it, Nick," he said aloud. "You're beginning to be a little single-minded on the subject of Pembroke."

He got to his feet and started back for camp. That scuba diver had been just some innocent naval historian, not Pembroke at all. He'd been excited about the pistol because it showed Drake really had anchored in Point Reyes. Everybody thought so, but nobody had actually proven it. The scuba diver wanted to find the frigate because that would be proof.

But that didn't make sense, either. Drake didn't *have* a frigate to have gotten wrecked in Point Reyes. He had started out from England with three ships, but by the time he'd rounded the bottom tip of South America only one was left, the *Golden Hind*. That hadn't been a frigate, and it hadn't been wrecked. It had gotten back to England with all its Spanish treasure intact.

So why did finding a pistol that had a Drake connection make the men believe they were close to finding some wrecked frigate?

Nick shrugged impatiently. That man in the boat had used the word *Drake* only once, and Nick was trying to make it the central fact. The important thing wasn't some tenuous link to Drake, but that somebody was wreck hunting in Point Reyes. And whoever it was didn't want other people to know. Nick was sure of that, remembering the tense, anxious way the scuba diver had scanned the shore for someone who might have overheard. Whoever was wreck hunting out there was doing it without official permission.

Wrecks in a national park would belong to the park. So would everything that was on them. Divers must be watched pretty carefully in a place like this with so many wrecked ships. So if there was treasure on a wreck, and you wanted it, you'd have to have a pretty good official reason to be scuba diving, to keep the authorities from watching what you brought up from the ocean bottom.

A scientific reason like doing underwater pollution research? It had been Pembroke who had organized the field trip. What perfect cover, if he wanted to dive for something illegal! With all those eminent researchers doing legitimate dives, no ranger would look twice at someone with motives other than research in mind.

Striding along the clifftop with the pebbles scattering down to the sea below, Nick shook his head. He didn't even know for sure that that diver *was* Pembroke. Even if it was, there might be some other explanation for the wreck hunting. The trouble was, Nick didn't want there to be another explanation. He wanted Pembroke to be a crook. He wanted to be the one to show Pembroke up. He couldn't trust his own logic, feeling like that.

Nick's hands clenched, then slowly relaxed. Those divers hadn't found what they were looking for. They would be back. All Nick had to do was keep an eye on the area they'd been searching, and eventually he'd see them again. And then, somehow, he'd find out if that diver really was Pembroke.

And if it was? Nick imagined Pembroke's photograph in the newspapers, the headlines screaming about misuse of conservation funds and criminal activity. He imagined himself on the witness stand, Pembroke with his head in his hands, the Conservocean Foundation in ruins, the *Leviathan* on the auction block.

Nick smiled, slow and hard. He'd need proof, of course. But that would come, if he watched long enough.

He had a whole summer, after all.

There were sounds in the calf's body. Anxiously, the mother listened. Echoes of thinnest echoes, the highest of high-pitched notes, things rubbing subtly inside, a wrongness.

Calfling? she called. *Calfling, will you feed?*

It would not. Lustrous eyes focused on her, first one large, dark pupil, then the other. Weeds swayed softly around its body. It was too thin.

She came closer, running her lips gently along its smooth head. Its taste was right, brine-faint and oily, full of life. Its full body was cool, and that was right, too. She nudged the calf surfaceward, watching for the color changes decreasing depth brought out in its skin: near black to violet to blue-green to gray. No hint of yellow, she thought, reassured, nothing of that grim, dusky red she had seen before in another calf, another time.

At the surface, she contracted her eye muscles, shaping her lens to make the maximum use of the light. *Let me see all of you,* she told the calf.

It stretched its own eye lens in mischievous imitation, lifted its flukes straight into the air, dropped its head below her own, and gurgled at her from underneath.

Play, the mother thought, even more reassured. She gave the nearest of the calf's flukes a warning tap with her flipper. *Lie still! Let me see!*

It rolled over, lying on its back, then its front. She scanned it quickly. Its skin was whole and taut, no scrapes or cuts to fester, nothing to worry about except that hint of boniness underneath.

If you would only feed! she scolded it.

It swam a circle around her flipper, then laid its cheek to hers, soft.

Silence, gentle as the sea.

There were no more noises in the calf's body.

I did not hear it, the mother told herself gladly. It was not there.

They dived, mother and baby, two shadows descending to a lightless world together.

CHAPTER NINE

IT WAS PAST SEVEN-THIRTY WHEN MARTY got the rowboat back to its mooring. She hauled it up the little cove as far as she could, replaced the Conservocean sign, and raced up the beach, sand spurting under her feet. The parking lot contained only a few more cars than usual. It was easy to see that the Nivens' blue van wasn't there, and Marty sighed with relief. Sam and Lynda must have stopped for dinner on the way back from San Francisco.

Her stomach growled at the thought, and she remembered that she had had nothing to eat since breakfast. She headed for camp. As she climbed, a radio went on. Over the clink of glasses, a static-filled male voice sang, "I know—a dark—secluded place." Marty entered the camp on "Ole," to see the photographer Janet Simpson doing an exaggerated, cheek-to-cheek tango with Heather Kent. Bill Lancaster, the diver who had been with Dr. Pembroke that day in the fog, was watching them and grinning, tapping out the rhythm on the beer can in his hand. At a large buffet table set up outside the dining tent Sheila Gough was filling a taco and talking continuously to Ann Duguay and Dr. Anderson. As the song on the radio came to an end, Marty heard her brisk voice saying, "Affecting the pelagic population more than I'd like." Nick was standing near them, reaching into a bowl of tortilla chips. If he had seen Marty come into the camp, he didn't show it.

She hesitated, but only for a moment. If he was going

to snub her, let him. She was too hungry to worry about it.

Dr. Duguay smiled at Marty as she joined them. "Did you have a nice day off?"

Dr. Anderson handed her an empty taco. "You must be starving. We were just about ready to send out a search party."

"It's a food-chain problem, I'm pretty sure," Dr. Gough said around a large mouthful of taco. Everyone looked at her. "With the cormorants, I mean," she explained. Dr. Anderson smothered a laugh.

Marty began to fill her taco. She was very aware of Nick standing silently beside her, dipping chips into a bowl of salsa. He seemed very separate from everything, but when Dr. Duguay's taco broke, he had a napkin in her hands before she could even look around for one; and later, when a moth began circling the burning candle someone had placed on the table, he blew the candle out before anyone else noticed. Marty saw the small, private smile he gave when the moth flew away. His face went all gentle, and his blue eyes were warm as a summer sky. Liking for him flooded her suddenly, followed by a pain so intense she had to turn her back. Nick didn't want anything from her. She didn't have anything to offer him, anyway. People who were smart and quick needed other smart, quick people. It was like Lynda and Sam, bright and witty and responsive to each other despite their wrangling, two puzzle pieces that matched.

"Anybody want a beer?" It was Heather Kent. She pulled two cans from a cooler and joined the group at the buffet table. "How about you, Nick?"

He looked uncomfortable. "Maybe later, thanks."

"Marty?" Heather offered politely. Marty shook her head. "Oh, yeah, I forgot, you're a minor, aren't you?"

"A minor what?" came Ray Pembroke's voice at the entrance of the dining tent. "I'll have that beer, Heather,

96

since it's going begging." He joined them, took the can from Heather's hand, and smiled down at Marty, his teeth very white. "Pretty quiet around here for a party. Those two little ones you look after in bed already?"

"They're in San Francisco," Marty said. She could feel Nick's stillness beside her. Ray Pembroke was standing right at his elbow.

"Nobody for you to watch," Pembroke said. He almost sounded teasing.

Her mind flashed to that first night, when he had caught her watching him. Was that what he meant? Or that other time, with his wineglass? But he had already turned to Nick. "How's that antique computer of Jonas's working out for you?"

"Fine," Nick said stonily.

"You write your own programs, do you?"

"That's right."

Pembroke didn't seem to notice Nick's aversion. He smiled. "If you program as well as you navigate in a fog, Jonas has got himself quite a research assistant. Where'd he find you, anyway?"

Somehow Dr. Anderson was standing between the two of them. He said, "Advertisements are wonderful little inventions, Ray. Speaking of which, I hear the latest fund-raising campaign's going great. A million dollars so far, isn't it?"

"A bit more, actually." Pembroke's voice was all at once clearer and sharper edged. "But a million dollars doesn't go very far when you have to lobby Washington."

"Conservocean doesn't do so badly with the politicians."

"That's because of Ray," Heather said. "In Washington, he *is* Conservocean. The politicians love him."

"We all love him," Janet Simpson said, dancing into hearing with Bill. "The man who made this summer possible."

Pembroke ignored her. "I just wish the politicians would love the issues," he said. "There are always one or two hot topics, but nobody in power gives a damn about most of the fundamental problems. Just mention the striped bass population of San Francisco Bay if you want to see a politician's eyes glaze. But the reason the bass is dying out is the same reason so much else is going wrong on the West Coast: the damming of the rivers, the selenium-poisoned runoff from land that should never have been irrigated in the first place, the fact that California farmers use 30 percent of all the pesticides applied in the United States—"

He really cares, Marty thought, and wondered why she was surprised.

"—and the whole mess swept under the carpet because the issue hasn't enough voter appeal. We can raise all kinds of money for acid rain or saving the whales, but—"

"Speaking of whales," Janet interrupted, "I saw a couple of spouts today."

Marty's hand tightened on her taco. It was stupid to have thought she could have the whales to herself. Obviously, she wouldn't have been the only person to see them, not on a marine field trip with so many trained observers.

Ann Duguay had heard Janet's interruption. She turned away from Dr. Gough. "I suppose they were humpbacks? They're seen fairly often here in the summer."

The photographer shrugged. "I only saw the spouts, and a bit of one back."

"Where were the spouts? A long way out?"

"No, just back of the surf line."

"Not humpbacks, then," Ann said eagerly, "and certainly not blues. Only the gray whale comes that close in." In the deepening twilight her hazel eyes sparkled. "Were the spouts heart shaped?"

"I didn't look at the shape. Sorry. There were two

spouts close together, and one was quite a bit smaller than the other. That's all I can tell you. I was taking photos of the surf off Limantour and caught the spouts a few times in my zoom."

"It's happened before," Ann said excitedly. "A mother and baby gray whale going north much later than the rest. Sometimes they'll even stay around a bay like this all summer and not go north at all. They were off Limantour, you say?"

"Closer to the mouth of Drake's Estero."

"When did you see the spouts?" Ann persisted.

Janet thought for a moment. "Just before noon, I'd say. Does it matter?"

"Only if they stayed around for a while. Did they?"

"I saw them off and on for about an hour, I guess. They didn't move very far."

"Feeding, probably. Maybe they really are staying in Drake's Bay for the summer." Ann's right hand clenched as if around an invisible pencil. "What a study opportunity! Glenna would get the data for her thesis. I could let people know at the San Diego conference next week, and Jamieson would hotfoot it over here, and Dougal and Shawna Turnbull. We'll keep that area near the Estero covered day and night. Once we have the whales tagged, we can—" She saw Marty's face. "Why, what's the matter, Marty?"

"I think—I'm sure—the whales have gone, Ann." She wasn't a good liar, but she had to try. She thought of the mother whale lifting her face into the sun, and that tide pool with its trapped and helpless inhabitants. Her chin went up. "I was out in the rowboat just before supper, and saw them swimming north, near Chimney Point. Every time they came up for air they were nearer to the point. I'm sure they were going away."

"Too bad, Ann," Ray Pembroke said. "It would have made a great addition to the field trip. But Marty's right.

I saw them too, at five-thirty. They were rounding Chimney Point, definitely leaving."

Desolation swept over Marty. Pembroke had seen the whales leave. Her lie had been true. The whales were gone. She wanted them free, but, oh, she didn't want them gone!

As quickly as it had descended, the desolation passed. The whales weren't gone. She was sure of it. Pembroke must have been mistaken about seeing the whales leave. They were still out in the bay, somewhere: She was as sure of it as she had been of Nick's safety that night in the fog.

She looked at Nick, who was staring at Pembroke. The iceberg aloofness in his eyes was gone, erased by a startled, blistering scorn. What had Pembroke done to make Nick react like that?

Ann Duguay gave a morose sigh. "I should have known I'd never get so lucky as to be in the same place at the same time as an anomalous gray whale pair." She added without much hope, "All the same, I think I'll ask around to see if anybody saw the whales earlier this week. If they were here more than just today, there's a chance they may be making this bay their headquarters. It might be worth our while to put a watch out in case they come back."

Marty didn't dare look at Nick's face. Five nights ago the whales had pushed his rowboat to shore. *Don't tell*, she willed him, staring at the long, thin fingers of his right hand, drumming at his thigh.

"I'd always heard you couldn't tag whales, anyway," Sheila Gough said.

"Oh, we don't really tag them," Ann said. "We just call it that. What we do is photograph them. They're all different from each other, you know. A good photo can identify individuals as easily as a name tag."

Marty heard this with mixed emotions. "You mean, you don't put some kind of radio or something on them, so that you always know where they are?"

"Not anymore. We just try to identify them when we

do see them again, that's all. It's not as useful for research, but it doesn't disturb them so much. God knows they deserve some respect from humans, after all we've done to them over the past."

"Hey," Heather protested, "is this a party or a seminar?" She called over to Tom MacKay's graduate student, who was fiddling with the radio, "Find something worth dancing to, Ian! Not that jazzy stuff, something with a beat. That's better. Come on, Ray, let's show these Canadians how to celebrate a national holiday!"

They danced off, laughing. After a moment Bill Lancaster put a smile on his face and whirled Janet away. Nick looked at Marty. "You want to dance?" he asked abruptly.

She hesitated, then nodded. Side by side, not touching, they moved away from the table. The music was fast, a Jerry Lee Lewis song, raunchy and loud and full of static. The rhythm was like pounding blood. They began to dance; strangers, not partners, apart from each other, isolated. Someone lit a Coleman lamp. Outside its circle of light the evening grew darker. Facing her, his face in shadow, Nick said softly, "Those whales haven't gone, have they?"

She jerked to a halt.

Nick put his hands on her shoulders. "Keep dancing," he said. "Don't look as if I said anything."

She obeyed. His hands stayed on her shoulders. She tried not to notice. "Are you saying I lied about seeing the whales leave?" she got out.

"I thought you might have. You looked like you were."

She bit her lip and said nothing.

"Marty, it's important. Did you lie, or didn't you?"

"They're so free," she said miserably. "I thought, if the scientists started studying them, they wouldn't ever be free again. They're special to me, Nick. They must be to you, too, or you would have told Ann about them pushing you to shore the other night."

"They're not special to me," he denied roughly. "I didn't tell because nobody would have believed me, that's all."

She only looked at him. He raised his chin. "It's true. I couldn't care less about those whales. They only matter because Pembroke said he saw them leave, too. And if he was where I think he was at five-thirty, he couldn't have. He was damn well lying."

Marty frowned puzzledly. "I thought he'd just made a mistake."

"Not him."

"Why would he lie?"

"Let's just say he might have his own reasons not to want a lot of people keeping watch on the area near the Estero."

Their feet moved, keeping the beat. Neither of them noticed.

"He didn't want us at the Estero, either," Marty said slowly. "Kathy and Junie and me, I mean. We saw him there, that first day. He and Bill were doing something with a—magnetometer. He said it was for pollution, but Lynda said it's mostly used for finding shipwrecks."

"That fits," Nick said grimly.

The music had changed. Their feet moved in time with it, smaller, slower steps bringing them closer together.

"Fits with what?"

"Someone named Ray was scuba diving at five-thirty tonight. That's Pembroke's first name, did you know? That Ray guy and another man were looking for a wrecked frigate near the Estero at five-thirty, not watching whales off Chimney Rock."

"You think it was Pembroke you saw at the Estero? But why would a fund-raiser be looking for shipwrecks?"

"Why does anybody?"

"To get treasure, you mean."

"To get *illegal* treasure, in this case. The contents of

shipwrecks found inside the boundaries of a national park belong to the government. There was a case in Florida a while back—I read about it in the newspaper. This guy was scuba diving, and by accident, just inside the boundary of a marine park, he found a wreck. When he tried to salvage it, the government took him to court. They hadn't known the wreck was there until he found it, but he couldn't get anything out of it without breaking the law. The government didn't even want to salvage the wreck, but it didn't want anybody else to have it. In the end the guy was so mad he printed the location of the wreck on place mats and used them in his restaurant, hoping somebody else would try to steal stuff from the wreck."

In his earnestness, his hands tightened on Marty's shoulders. "It'll be the same thing here," he went on. "Anybody diving for a wreck has to be doing it illegally. And don't you see what a perfect cover this whole field trip must be for someone who wants to dive for treasure without the rangers getting nervous?"

It did make sense. But Marty wasn't sure. Nick wanted Pembroke to be the one doing something illegal, because he blamed Pembroke for his brother's death. And when you wanted something badly enough, you could make anything seem reasonable. "What are you going to do?" she asked at last.

"I haven't got any proof. It'd be his word against mine, if I said anything now. Anyway, until he finds the wreck, he won't have done anything illegal. I'll watch him, but I have to spend so much time at the computer . . ." His voice trailed away.

"I'll watch him, too," Marty offered, "when I can."

"Thanks." His blue eyes searched hers. Almost inconsequentially he said, "You have taco sauce on your face."

She couldn't stop looking at him. "Where?"

He touched the corner of her mouth lightly with his

index finger. "There." He rubbed briefly. "All gone." He smiled.

His hand went back to her shoulder. They danced, his hands warm on her T-shirt, hers dangling uncertainly by her sides. The static on the radio cleared. "Annie's Song" was playing, wordless and soft, the cascade of guitar notes making one melody, the flute another. Different, yet the same; working together for their meaning. The flute sang higher, hauntingly sweet. *La la-la-la laa, lum*. Distant as time, Marty seemed to hear another song, something bigger than "Annie's Song," something that contained that song in the same way "Annie's Song" contained the guitar and the flute. An echo, she thought dreamily, and clasped her hands against the small of Nick's back.

It was nothing she decided to do; they seemed to have done it on their own. His hands left her shoulders and slid down her back, following the fall of her hair. Thighs brushing thighs, blood thrumming steady and hot from the heart, the soft, slow, slide of hair and hands. There was no space between them. They matched, the music was their meeting place, opposites with one edge. The ancient beat was inside them, a pattern too distant for the ear to hear. They echoed it, listening with their bodies.

A small hand tugged at Marty's forearm. "Marty, look at my Band-Aid!"

Marty blinked. Kathy's voice?

"I got it at McDonald's," Kathy said importantly. "I bleeded all over their floor."

Nick's hands fell away; there was a cold spot on Marty's back where they had been.

"Don't bother Marty, Kathy," Sam's voice called.

It was too late. The music had stopped, and Nick was gone.

CHAPTER TEN

SUNDAY WAS NICK'S DAY OFF. HE WAS gone from camp before anyone else was up, hiking in the early morning sunshine to the main road, where he hitched a ride with a rancher to a café in Point Reyes Station. There he demanded coffee from the sleepy-eyed waitress, plunked himself down at a corner table, and tried to read the newspaper. Huge, dark eyes stared out at him from every page. He slammed the paper shut.

It had been one dance!

He gulped down his coffee, dug out a quarter for the waitress, and left the newspaper where it was. Outside, a cooling breeze blew his hair back from his forehead. He strode along the highway to the narrow bridge crossing Lagunitas Creek. The sunlight shone through a eucalyptus leaf floating in the thready stream, turning it the shiny sugar red of Marty's hair.

Pembroke would be up by now. He might even be over at the Estero. While Nick mooned over a dried-up leaf, Pembroke might already be smiling down at the first artifact of the illegally salvaged frigate.

Richard wouldn't have understood the way Nick was acting. Richard always knew what was important. If he liked a girl, he got her. That was that, and over with as quickly. There was always another one waiting. And meanwhile his studying went on, and his solitary camping trips, his sit-ins and his guitar practice, his search for the world's best fudge. Once Richard decided he had to do something, nothing ever stopped him from doing it. Certainly not any girl.

And Nick, who last night had made a vow to watch Pembroke, had let his fear of seeing Marty again make him break that vow only a few hours later.

He couldn't really be so afraid of her, could he?

A dairy truck was making a slow turn onto Sir Francis Drake Boulevard. Its windows were open. Nick hailed it. "Going anywhere near Drake's Bay?"

The driver leaned toward the passenger window. "Eh?"

"Can you give me a lift to Drake's Bay?"

"The turnoff suit you? I'm going on toward the point, myself."

Nick ran and pulled open the door. He would have to go back to camp to get food and his binoculars and a camera, but if he saw Marty, he wouldn't let her affect him. Last night, there had been the worry about not being able to find her, and then, all that stuff about the whales reminding him of that other time he had turned to her in the dimness of a Coleman-lit night, that other time he had told her things, his fingers stroking her hair. Great, dark, lustrous eyes watching him from the shadows; like those whale eyes out in the fog, eyes that should not have been able to show compassion, yet did, that offered him what he didn't need and didn't dare want.

It was all a trick of the light and the music, Nick told himself, settling into the seat of the truck. He grinned mechanically at the driver and slammed the door a little too hard behind him. In daylight, she'd be nothing but a tall, skinny kid with a bony face.

The mother was still, using her flippers only enough to keep her blowholes in the air. Skin to skin with her, the calf drowsed in the warm sunlight, water drops glistening on its back. It was singing in its sleep. Rasps of sound, snuffles, murmurs, whoops. The mother's great sounding board of a body resonated to those small sounds of life beside her.

The sea hummed a larger harmony: the gurgle of the distant surf, stones grating on the ocean floor, the clink and snap of hard-back life in the eelgrass, the crunch of toothed jaws on protesting shells. Water-breathers made endless silver streams of hiccuping, bubbling metabolism. Other creatures darted and swirled, see-through blobs swishing up their own currents, squids battling for dominance, worms writhing and sponges swaying and shells squeaking open and shut, the soft squirt of new life. The mother listened and the sounds imprinted on her body, comfortable images, unalarming.

From somewhere past the trailing eelgrass she identified dolphins, with their chatter and click. She listened carefully to the click-speech, though she knew this was more a method of hunting than song. Dolphins could sing, though they preferred fast swimming, and hunting tricks, and play. The mother thought about them, racing their way gloriously through the light-spangled water. She thought of singing out to them, to see if they would stop. But they would have no songs for her. No news of her own People, gone so long into the north, leaving her and her calf behind.

For some time after the dolphins were gone, the mother lay sleepless. She wasn't hungry, and she wasn't tired. Her mind roamed free, boundless as the sea. She let it go where it would, even onto the land where the two-legged ones were.

There were two there that interested her. The young male, of course; she had not seen him since that night she had pushed his log to shore. *Had* that been obedience to the Song, or her own addition to it? She had pondered it many times, since her nursling calf had asked.

And that other two-legged one, the female. Not of the People, her song alien, yet still the mother responded to her with an instinct as warm and ancient as rushing milk. An oddness, there. Too much harmony. It disturbed her, even as it drew her.

The young female was near, but asleep. The male was far away, his song a thread. The mother turned her mind again to the sea.

Deep, deep, in the farthest distance, came the sustained, low moan of the largest of the People, the great Blue. It was too far away for one of the mother's size to answer. She could only listen. It sang of solitary journeys through waters warm or lidded with crack-ice, of the endless, futile searches for companionship, of the ache of an empty womb. Hearing, the mother moved a little closer to her own calf, brushing her flipper over its sleeping form to feel the life in it.

After all, there were worse kinds of loneliness than to be a mother alone with her calf while all the rest of her own People were far away in the north.

Marty woke late on Sunday. A lot of people were eating breakfast when she went down to the washroom, but by the time she got back, only Ann Duguay remained.

"Lyn said to tell you good-bye," Ann said. "She's spending the day working with Ewan and Janet at Double Point. You want some coffee?" She gestured invitingly at the seat next to her.

Marty poured herself a cup and sat down. "Where are the kids?"

"Off with Sam. There's a great second-hand bookstore in Point Reyes Station."

"Junie's idea, right?" Marty said, smiling.

"How did you guess?" Ann smiled in return.

108

For a while they drank coffee in companionable silence. Then Ann said, "What're you up to today?"

"I don't know." Marty thought of the whales. If only there were some way she could get near them, instead of just waiting and hoping they would come near her! And then there was Nick. Would he think, if she stayed around the camp all day, that she was waiting there hoping for him to notice her? And where was he, anyway? She chewed her lip. "I wish it wasn't Sunday."

"Me too," Ann said vehemently. "A beautiful diving day, and me stuck here in camp. I know Glenna has to have some time off, but when a job needs two people—and it's not even hard work, basically just sitting in the boat and getting a tan! When *I* was a graduate student—" She broke off again, and laughed. "Listen to me! Don't I sound the crochety old slave driver!"

"I could sit in the boat while you dive, if that's all you need," Marty surprised herself by saying. "Unless—well, I don't know how to scuba—I don't even snorkel—so if you got into trouble diving—"

"You can pull a rope, can't you? And you could always row for help, if necessary. That's the main thing, not to dive alone. Mind you, I was simplifying things a bit when I said that was all Glenna would do. She'd have to follow my signals and write down some numbers as well."

Marty reached for a piece of bread. With her face averted, she said, "I'm not smart like Glenna."

Ann regarded her thoughtfully. "There's more than one kind of smart."

"Not in school. In school there's only one." Carefully, Marty spread butter on the bread, then some jam.

"School isn't everything," Ann said after a minute. Marty looked up at her, startled. "No, really. I've had graduate students who never got less than an *A* in their life and were absolutely useless at thinking. And I've had assistants right out of high school who never got more

109

than a *D* and were creative as little Einsteins. More and more I'm wondering what it is that schools really test." She tossed back her coffee, grinned at Marty, and said, "Now then, would you really like to help me today, or were you just being polite?"

Marty thought about being out in a boat again, a whole day this time, not just for a few hours. Closer to the whales, the way she had wished; and far enough away from Nick that he wouldn't think she was hanging around camp just to be with him. "I—well, if you really think I can do it—"

"Great. We'll go as soon as you've finished your breakfast."

While Marty ate, Ann explained what they were going to do. She was working with a small group of sea lions ("a harem," she said cheerfully) who had grown accustomed to her presence enough to go about their own business and ignore her. When one of the sea lions dived, she would dive with it, measuring the length of time it stayed underwater and the depth of its dive, and taking a sample of the water for later analysis. Then she would signal the numbers to Marty in the boat, who'd write them down and read the current ozone count from an instrument in the boat.

Marty tried to listen, but thoughts of the whales kept intruding. I'll be out on the water, she thought. Near the whales again. This time I won't fall asleep. This time, when the whales come—

"—do a statistical analysis," Ann said. "Correlations . . . negatively affecting lung capacity."

Maybe she shouldn't hope to see them after all, not with Ann there too. Maybe—

"I said, are you ready?" Ann said, smiling at her quizzically.

Marty blushed and nodded. She'd missed something, obviously. Probably it was some important thing she was

110

supposed to do on the boat. And then she wouldn't know how, because she hadn't been paying attention.

Ann could talk all she liked about research assistants with *D*'s. She'd probably never in her whole life had to work with anybody who was really dumb.

Nick tossed a bit of bread crust to a gull soaring in the thermals between cliff and sea. The bird caught it neatly, and with a few lazy flaps of its wings dropped to the top of the sand dune beside him. "You want more, do you?" Nick muttered. "Well, don't we all?"

He had sand in his shoes and there were pins and needles in his legs from sitting still for so long. The last drop of water in his canteen had gone long ago. He had dropped his camera in the mud that lined the Estero and the film wouldn't advance. He was in a foul mood.

All he had to show for his Sunday off was a broken camera. The same rubber dinghy he'd seen yesterday had roared by, once, just after noon. Nick had grabbed his binoculars, but it took him too long to focus; the boat was gone before he could see who was in it. And then, about five minutes later, another boat had appeared near the mouth of the Estero, rowing slowly along the shore of the bay. And in the boat was Marty.

What was she doing out there? He had told her Pembroke might be searching for the frigate here. She must have known he wouldn't come if there were witnesses. She was ruining any chance Nick might have of getting the evidence he needed. Nick almost stood up behind his sand dune and yelled at her. He was glad he didn't, when a few minutes later a wet-suited Ann Duguay surfaced a little way in front of the rowboat.

"He's going into the Estero, I think," Ann called.

He? Nick thought. Was there another diver down there?

"Should we follow him?" Marty asked, in her soft, clear voice.

"I don't think so. There's a harbor seal colony in there that's really touchy about humans. It'd be interesting to see what they'd make of our sea lion, but I don't think we'll intrude. Anyway, I'm too tired. You must be, too. I'd never have believed a small sea lion would swim that far. Sorry."

A sea lion, not a diver, Nick thought.

Ann stripped off her tanks and gave them to Marty. Then she scrambled into the rowboat. Through the binoculars, Nick watched her run a finger down the clipboard Marty handed her, then smile and pat Marty's shoulder. He thought he heard a "Fine job, Marty." Then, for a long while they just sat and talked, Ann in the bow with her back turned to Nick, Marty in the stern with the oars, keeping the boat facing into the shore. Now and then they ate something. Whenever Ann said something, Marty got that intent look that he had noticed in her right from the first, head tilted to one side so that her long hair brushed the bottom boards of the boat, big eyes deep and focused and looking as if they could see more things than other people.

Nick found he couldn't stop staring at her face. He had thought it was too bony; through the binoculars, he saw that he had been wrong. The bones were high and sharp, but there was a warmth in the shadows they cast. She had a wide, soft mouth whose smile extended exactly to the edge of those shadows. It balanced her, that smile. It gave lights to her dark eyes, too. He hadn't noticed her skin, before. In the strong noon light he saw that it was perfectly smooth and the same color all over, an ivory paleness that defied the sun. She looked untouched.

Once, while Ann was poring a second time over the clipboard, Marty turned her head sharply, staring out over the bay as if she had heard something. In profile her face went suddenly so longing and anxious that Nick swept the binoculars in the direction she was looking. There was nothing there. A moment later he saw a spout. Another. So the whales were out there. How had she known to look in that direction, at just that moment?

The sun was setting. Nick got stiffly to his feet. He should have known Pembroke wouldn't come back today. Ann and Marty had sat there just that much too long. Their rowboat would have been in plain view from the *Leviathan*. Even after Marty had finally started to row again, they didn't go very far before they headed for shore, and this time they hauled the boat right up on the beach. A long few minutes passed with them out of Nick's field of view. When they finally reappeared, both Marty and Ann were wearing wet suits. They waded out into the surf, and Ann handed Marty a snorkel tube. She said something; Marty listened, nodding several times. Ann spit into her goggles; Marty did the same. She ducked under the water; so did Marty. Beyond a doubt, Ann Duguay was teaching Marty how to snorkel.

She was a fast learner, Nick thought, an hour later. She'd be able to snorkel as far as she wanted soon, on her own. An hour after that, and she was. She swam out a long way, not lifting her head even when she rested, then snorkeling on some more. She didn't stop until Ann swam after her and yelled. Nick was sure she had been going in the direction of the whale spouts.

Tramping back along the beach in the waning light, Nick tried to figure out why he was so disturbed. The only thing that came to him, insistent and clear, was the memory of Marty's voice last night, saying, "They're special to me, Nick."

The whales were special to her, and now she could snorkel.

It bothered him how strongly the two things were linked in his mind.

113

CHAPTER ELEVEN

THE COMPUTER WAS BEEPING. NICK stared at the screen. What now? No error message, and not the battery packs. So why the beep? He pressed the ENTER key. The beep came again. Save your work, he told himself suddenly. That's what the beep meant, save your work. He had programmed it himself to remind him; how could he have forgotten?

Outside the tent he could hear the drone of Lynda Niven's voice. On and on, all that long Monday afternoon: He'd never known anybody who could read aloud that long. But then, he'd never known anybody who had to entertain a moderately sick Junie Niven, either.

Marty had been given the day off. "It's not that I don't trust you, Marty," Lyn had said at breakfast. "But Kathy's got a pretty high fever, and with Junie complaining as well, it'd be too much to ask of any sitter. I'll stay with them—it's what I'd do if we were in Vancouver. Unless maybe Sam would like to—"

"No way," Sam said. "I had them all day yesterday."

"Pig," Lyn said, making a face at him.

"Pig yourself," he replied. "I've got to get *some* work done this summer."

"It's probably your doing they're sick at all. You would let them play with that germy little baby in Golden Gate Park on Saturday."

Sam leaned over the table and planted a huge, wet kiss on Lyn's mouth. "Some more lovely germs for you, sweetheart," he crooned. "Take them back to the kids for me, will you?" He was gone before Lyn could hit him.

"I really wouldn't mind looking after them, Lyn," Marty had said.

But Lynda was adamant. "No, you have some fun. Go snorkeling again, why don't you? Ann says you're a natural. Keep it up, and you'll be scuba diving before the end of the summer."

Nick must have made a movement of protest, because Marty looked at him. "I don't have a wet suit," she said slowly.

Lyn smiled. "I brought my old wet suit for a spare, and haven't used it once. It'd fit you, I'm sure. Why don't you just keep it until I ask for it back? It's in the tent. Oh, damn, there's Kathy crying again." She whirled away.

Now Marty and Nick were alone at the table except for Dr. Anderson, who was absorbed in a statistics manual. "I could spend the day at the Estero, Nick," she offered softly, "you know, to see if Dr. Pembroke comes?"

It was the first reference either of them had made to Saturday night, when Nick had taken her into his confidence about the search for the frigate. Last night he had been going to ask her if she'd seen who was in the motorboat that had whizzed by her at the Estero at noon, but he couldn't figure out how, without admitting he had been watching her. And then she'd gone to bed frustratingly early, and he couldn't ask her at all.

Now she came out with it of her own volition. "Dr. Pembroke did come to the Estero yesterday," she said, keeping her voice so low that Nick had to lean close to hear it. "He didn't stay, though. Just came, and saw Ann and me, and left again. He might go back today, if he thinks no one is there. I could watch."

Nick couldn't help himself. "You'd have to stay hidden. That means out of the water. Definitely no snorkeling."

She hesitated, and suddenly Nick was angry. "I guess it just depends what's important, eh? A chance of getting close to those whales that're so *special* to you, or of finding the evidence that Pembroke's a crook. Just keep in mind that it might be a hell of a lot better for the whales if Pembroke never saw them again."

She tilted her head, her long hair swinging forward. He jerked away before it could brush his hand. Irrationally, he thought of seaweed.

"Were you at the Estero yesterday, Nick?" she asked suddenly. "Did you see the whales? Did you see—me?"

"I . . . well, yes, I did. But it wasn't—I was watching out for Pembroke. I wasn't spying on you." But he had been. He had spent all that time looking through the binoculars at her face. Desperately, he went on. "I had no idea you'd even be there."

She looked at him, her eyes dark as deep pools. "Why did you say Pembroke shouldn't see the whales again?"

"If he knew they were still around the area he wants to search, he might be afraid someone else would see them, too. He wouldn't want all those scientists hanging around the Estero. He might think it would be worth his while to prevent that."

"Prevent it? How?"

"Well, he might—get rid of them. The whales, I mean."

She gave a startled gasp, almost a wheeze. Dr. Anderson looked up from his manual. "Gesundheit. You're not getting sick, too, are you, Marty?"

"No," she said. "No."

He eyed the two of them, nodded abruptly, and said, "Think I left something in my tent."

When he was gone, Marty said, "Nick, Pembroke believes in *saving* the whales. He wouldn't—"

"All I'm saying," Nick interrupted, "is that if those

whales have got any brains at all, they'll stay as far away from Pembroke as they can. Richard didn't, and look what happened to him."

"But that's—I mean, it's not the same thing, is it? Pembroke didn't kill Richard. Not really kill; I mean, being on his ship when a bomb exploded isn't the same thing as—"

He glared at her furiously. "That's what everybody says. I'm irrational. Pembroke's an angel. The world is unfolding as it should. And nobody kills whales anymore. Don't worry, be happy." He gave a savage laugh, then looked down at his hands, white knuckled, on the table.

She sat as still as stone, saying nothing, hardly even breathing. He had never been more aware of anybody in his life. After a long moment, without looking up, he muttered, "It's just—oh, Marty, just don't let those whales matter to you."

"It's too late," she said. "They already do."

He was busy with Dr. Anderson when she left, and couldn't see if she took the wet suit with her, or even in what direction she went. But all day, sitting in front of the computer, he kept messing up, entering the wrong numbers, erasing good data, spending half his time getting unnecessary cups of coffee and listening to the monotone of Lynda Niven's voice.

He wanted Marty on dry land. He wanted her safe. He wanted . . . Savagely, he pounded the keyboard. What did it matter what he wanted unless she wanted it, too?

The computer beeped again. FILE TOO LARGE, the screen said. Damn! He shoved back his chair. He needed some air. Today was a write-off, anyway.

Outside the tent Lynda's voice was clearer. " 'Don Francisco Zararte was bound for Peru with a cargo of silk, porcelain, and other goods from China. On the fourth of

April—' Heavens, Junie, this is boring. Haven't you had enough of Drake's conquests by now?"

Nick had been heading for the overlook, but the word *Drake* stopped him in his tracks.

"I want to know about the harbor in Point Reyes," Junie whined. "Doesn't it say anything about that?"

"Let me see. This next bit is just Zararte's report. 'I went up to Drake and kissed his hands. He received me with a good countenance and took me to his cabin, where he said, "I am a very good friend to those who deal with me truly, but to those who do not—' " Blah-blah-blah. Same old charming Drake. 'He assured me that my life and ship were safe. Water, he said, was what he wanted. He spoke much of the death of a friend of his called Thomas Doughty.' Nothing here about Point Reyes. You want me to stop?"

"Wasn't Thomas Doughty the guy Drake decapitated?"

"Who remembers? Seems to me he's been doing nothing but mayhem ever since I woke up this morning."

"It *was* Doughty, I remember. He and Drake had a banquet together, and then Drake chopped off his head. And Drake called him his friend. Read the rest."

"My voice is just about worn out, Junie."

"Come on, Mom. My eyes are sore, but I'll read it myself if—"

"Not so loud, you'll wake Kathy. You're sure you don't want some Rachel Carson for a change? Okay, on with the blood and gore. 'The dead man's brother was on the ship. He dined at Drake's table but did not speak nor did others speak to him. He never left the ship as others did. I enquired of the crew if Drake had private enemies but I heard of none. All agreed that their general, as they call him, was adored.' "

There was more, but Nick briefly stopped listening, thinking of John Doughty, sitting silent at the captain's table for all those thousands of miles. When he tuned in again, Lynda was reading. " 'He took from me certain pieces of Chinese porcelain and begged me to excuse him.' Chinese porcelain. Hmm. That would be Ming dynasty, unless my history's all wrong. My, what a strange bird that Drake was! Imagine stealing priceless Ming porcelain and asking the victim's forgiveness!"

"Right over the edge," Junie agreed, with an audible yawn.

"Don't tell me you're finally getting tired."

"You still haven't got to the part where the *Golden Hind* gets to Point Reyes."

"One more paragraph. If it isn't mentioned there, you'll just have to wait. Where am I now? Oh, yeah. 'His crew is about eighty in number, fifty fighting men, the rest craftsmen and boys. I believe no vessel can overtake him. I think he is the greatest sailor who ever lived.' And that's that. No blood and gore after all. Now go to sleep."

Nick went thoughtfully back to his computer. Funny to think of Drake coming out with the story of Thomas Doughty to a Spanish prisoner of war. Almost as if something inside him were forcing him to talk. And then begging the Spaniard's forgiveness for stealing the Ming porcelain! Weird how that Spaniard seemed to almost *like* Drake. Junie was right; the whole thing was right over the edge.

Ming porcelain. Something tickled at his brain. He left the computer again and got out the book Dr. Anderson had lent him. He went to the index. Here it was, page 189. Detailed account by Alderman Richard Martyn, Francis Drake, and Christopher Harris of the treasure Drake brought back to England. Silver bullion, 22,899 pounds. Coarse silver, 512 pounds, 6 ounces. Gold bullion, 101 pounds, 10 ounces. Some spices and silks, a few bits of jewelry.

Nick had remembered correctly. There was no mention

of any porcelain. Drake had stolen priceless Ming porcelain from that Spaniard, and he hadn't brought it back to
England.

So where was it?

It was past midnight. The camp on the bluffs was still.
Moonlight poured its white magic down on the little tents,
softening the edges of things. There was no wind. Even
the distant surf seemed barely to sigh.

It was cool in her tent, but Marty lay on top of her
sleeping bag, unnoticing. Her hands were behind her head,
wrapped in her hair; her knees were bent. She wore only
a nightgown, a thin, silvery nylon thing, totally inappro-
priate for camping. She could feel every fold of it against
her skin. In the moonlight coming through her window
flap she could see her own body shimmering beneath the
nylon. It had an odd, remote beauty, like something seen
through clear water a long way away.

And yet. And yet.

One hand left her hair, running lightly along her leg,
knee to thigh, then up her abdomen, slowly over the
slippery nylon, slowly to her chest. Her fingers trailed a
warm, close darkness, an ache.

She had not swum with the whales today.

She had listened to Nick and stayed out of the water.

She had watched for Pembroke at the Estero and seen
him come with the man Bill, and they had dived and swum
all day and not found anything; nor had they seen the
whales she, Marty, had been so careful to will away.

I want them, she thought.

And still her hand moved lightly over the strangeness
of her own body, painting soft, dark ropes to keep her
here in camp, in the tent so near to Nick's.

I want.

The wetsuit lay beside her. She let her free hand touch
it. Its cold, rubbery feel alienated her. How odd that she

must wear it to float free, when a simple nylon gown, or nothing at all, could tie her to her own body.

The moonlight shifted. She got to her feet and stripped off the nightgown. There was enough talcum powder in the wet suit from the last time Lynda had worn it; it slid easily over her body. She debated over the helmet and decided, in the end, to leave it behind. When she left the tent she didn't bother with a flashlight; the moon was bright enough for anything. She wore her sneakers and the wet suit, nothing else, and her hair rippled behind her like a shimmering nylon ghost.

Nick didn't know what awakened him. One moment he was asleep, dreamless; the next, his eyes were open, peering into moonlight. Across the tent Dr. Anderson was a motionless lump beneath the covers, soundless as the night. Nothing there to have jerked him awake like this. But something had. What? He lay still, listening hard. He told himself to turn over and go back to sleep, but he couldn't. Eyes toothpick-wide, he stared into the moonlight, waiting. At last he heard the sound of a tent door being unzipped.

Marty's.

It could have been anyone's, of course. Someone who had to go down to the washroom in the middle of the night. Nick knew it wasn't. Quietly, he slid out of his bag, pulled on a pair of jeans and a sweater, and headed for his own door. For a long moment he made himself wait so she wouldn't hear him unzipping his own door. When he got out, she was gone.

Instinctively, he began following the trail leading down to the Visitors' Center. The moonlight was disturbingly bright. When he was only halfway down he saw her, a slim darkness surrounded with light, hair flying behind. She was leaping the little creek that bisected the beach.

He could see that she wore a wet suit and was heading for the ocean.

He couldn't call out. Her name strangled in his throat. It was that day at the bus all over again, Richard climbing up and holding on to the door, yelling something funny about wet-blanket good-byes, and he himself choking with words he couldn't say: Don't go, I'll manage just fine without you, Don't leave me, If that's what you want, who needs you, anyway? And the day of the funeral, lying on his bed silent and motionless and staring at the ceiling, letting his parents go without a word of response to any of their pleas.

Words were no good.

Caring was no good.

And the surf hissed, and the moonlight gleamed against Marty's head bobbing against the still waters, out and farther out until there was no way to distinguish it from that of any other swimming mammal, and still Nick watched and waited. And then there were three heads, not one, and Marty was swimming with the whales.

It was like nothing she had ever known. Hair and baleen mingled, swaying softly in currents they made themselves. Movement like a dance, like music heard far off, bodies brushing, faces, hand-to-fin, gentle. The calf played joyously, a little too rough; Marty gasped for air, and the mother's fin encircled her and raised her up, infinitely careful. She could rest there. Weightless, tiny as an infant, safe, her fingers went out and stroked the great, cold body beside her, and it was not alien, it was pulsing with life and soft, softer than human skin, and there was love in it, love for Calfling and for Marty herself, love for a world of clean air and clean water, love for the Song within herself, love for the song within them all.

I love you, Marty said.

So sings the Song, said the mother.

And the mother swam on the surface, slowly, and Marty swam beside her in the arc of one fin, and Calfling in the other, and they did not dive, but breathed the same air, their meeting place.

CHAPTER TWELVE

FOR THE NEXT FIVE DAYS, NICK SAW A great deal of Marty, but always at a distance, hurrying in and out of the Nivens' big tent with trays of food and tissue boxes, searching the van for lost toys, once lugging in a huge goldfish bowl someone had brought for the invalids. After the first day, Junie and Kathy felt well enough for Lynda to leave them with Marty, but still their sneezes reverberated through the camp. "No leaving the tent until both your fevers are gone," Lynda said, "and even then, not until this rotten weather clears. If it ever does."

Thick as a frog in the throat, fog had again settled in over Point Reyes. By noon on Tuesday it was impossible to see from one tent to the next, and the Fourth of July celebrations were confined to a small party in the dining tent. Nick knew Marty would be staying with Junie and Kathy, and he remained at his computer, working by the light of the Coleman lantern. The music from the dining tent distracted him. He told himself to ignore it, but it wouldn't leave him alone, strong and disturbing, an urgent beat pulsing steadily through the fog. Whatever deep bass notes accompanied it, he found he was continually straining to hear the melody.

And whatever numbers or words filled the computer screen in front of him, it was Marty's wet-suited body he saw in front of him, lines and curves and the flying silk of her hair, moonlight shaped, beautiful.

At noon on Thursday Nick came to the end of the great

124

pile of data Dr. Anderson had collected. The weather was still misty, but most of the scientists had gotten back to their projects. Nick knew that more yellow pads of data would be waiting for him on the card table tonight. But for now he had a few clear hours. The red-and-white dinghy wasn't in its usual position on the *Leviathan*'s deck, and Nick hesitated between rowing the discharged batteries over to the ship while the chance of running into Pembroke was less, and going to the Estero to see if Pembroke was there. In the Nivens' tent he could hear Marty and Kathy singing "Oh, They Built the Ship *Titanic*," with Junie chiming in at the chorus. No sneezes today. By tomorrow, maybe, Marty could get away from those two kids long enough for him to—

He shook the thought away. He would get the trip to the *Leviathan* over with quickly and then go down to the Estero. Pembroke would be sure to be there, taking advantage of the break in the weather. No one could have gone diving during the worst of the fog this week.

Nick took the discharged battery packs and headed off down the tarmac. Marty and Kathy were singing the last verse as he left.

> "Oh, the moral of this story, as you can
>   plainly see,
> Is to wear a life preserver when you go
>   out to sea."

He couldn't get the tune out of his mind. All the way over to the *Leviathan*, while water lapped against the rowboat's bow, the words repeated like a broken record. Wear a life preserver. Out to sea. He dug in with the oars, careful not to splash. Wear a life preserver. Small waves, gray as the sky. Not like that other night, when the water had been like shot silk. It was just here that Marty had swum out to find the whales. Here, yes, right here, she had found them.

Marty hadn't worn a life preserver. Marty had worn nothing but a wet suit.

Somehow he was at the *Leviathan*'s ladder. A crewman greeted him; he nodded back. People took his visits for granted by now. He didn't, but there were ways to get through everything. Ten strides from the ladder to the companionway, eight steps down, fifteen more strides to the office with Ray Pembroke's name on the door (turning his head to avoid looking at it), then five more to the computer room, closing its door firmly behind him, and finally, a deep breath in the familiar, electronic setting. He had always managed to avoid running into Pembroke; he didn't know how.

The mist was worsening again when he moored the dinghy back at Drake's Beach. He ran the fresh battery packs up to his tent, grabbed the camera he'd borrowed from Paul Wilson and a fresh roll of film, and was gone from camp again without seeing anyone. He took the clifftop route to the Estero. As he had guessed, the red-and-white dinghy from the *Leviathan* was moored in Drake's Bay just outside the entrance to the channel. Nick crept up to the edge of the bluffs without the man in the boat seeing him. It would have been hard for him to see Nick through the mist, anyway. Nick himself had to stare for a long time to be sure that the red-shirted man sitting down there, slack armed and bored looking, was Bill Lancaster. Nick took a picture of him with what he hoped would be the telltale hook of the Estero sandspit in the foreground. But with the fog worsening the way it was, how much of the photo would turn out was impossible to guess. Anyway, it would be useless as proof of illegal activity. Still, it felt better than doing nothing.

After a long time Pembroke surfaced, but the fog had gotten so bad that Nick almost missed him. It was Bill's scarlet shirt moving from one side of the boat to the other that alerted him. With Bill leaning over the side, the two men talked. Nick hoped the fog would help him to hear, but only a few words came clear: "Tello," he thought one was; and "Archives of the Indies." After a long and undecipherable mutter, a complete sentence rewarded him: "I told you, it wouldn't have been worth as much in Drake's time, so if he had to abandon something, it'd be that." Then another mutter, incomprehensible.

That? That what? Nick could have yelled in frustration.

The worsening fog clearly worried the two men. Nick got a very blurry snap of Ray Pembroke coming aboard; it would look like a snowman in a blizzard, Nick knew. Then the little dinghy's motor roared into action, heading for the *Leviathan*. Nick guessed they were trying to get back while they could still see. He supposed he had better do the same.

All this waiting and watching, he thought, trudging back along the clifftop. What if the summer went by, and nothing came of it all? What if he was never able to show the world that Pembroke was a fraud and a liar and a thief?

It wouldn't come to that. It couldn't. There was too much riding on it. Nick would get Pembroke because he had to.

It was as simple as that.

On Friday morning the fog was gone. Marty knew it as soon as she opened her eyes. The dawn light in her tent was different, a heavy brightness that weighed down on her like too many blankets. She leaped out of her sleeping bag. All week she had waited for this: no fog, and some time free from Junie and Kathy. She stripped off her nightgown, powdered herself all over, and began to pull on the wet suit. The whales were out in the bay.

Sometimes in the last five days she had felt as if only the surface of her were there in the camp on the top of the bluffs. Playing Monopoly, throwing out messy tissues, looking for a purple crayon for Kathy or some book Junie simply had to have right that minute, it was her body that carried her through, gentler than usual but automatic, kinder because of something absent within her that had to be made up for. She heard people talk to her, and she answered them, but all such voices seemed dimmed as if by music in the foreground, cadences and tonalities and sweet, winding rhythms, repeating and expanding and dying, though never entirely. It was whalesong she danced to, inwardly, dreamily; and then her body was only a surface, and she was weightless. But now and then something made her look at Nick: holding his cereal spoon at breakfast with those long, thin fingers that she wanted, stupidly, to touch; or making that shoulder-swinging walk of his down to the rowboat, blue-jeaned legs long and tight; or early in the morning, coming tousle haired up from the washrooms. And then her weight returned, thudding like an elevator drop, heavy darkness within her, an ache she didn't want to stop.

Someone was scratching at her tent door. "Aren't you up yet, Marty?" Kathy's voice, trying to whisper. "Mom says we're not sick anymore. Hey, Marty! You want to come for a swim before breakfast?"

She was standing half dressed in the middle of her tent. Seven o'clock. How could it be seven o'clock, when a minute ago it had been only six?

"Marty?"

"Coming, Kathy." Slowly, she slid out of the wetsuit. Slowly, she put on her old pink bathing suit. A swim before breakfast, splashing and yelling kids, sand castles and duck dives. The whales wouldn't come now.

She had had her chance, and she had wasted it.

The sky was the color of an old bruise, yellowish violet. People commented on it at breakfast, and on the strange, heavy heat that had replaced the cold of the fog. "This weather is straight out of the bayou," Heather said, wiping her forehead with one hand and passing around the mail with the other. "Who'd try to run a camp in Point Reyes? Nick, there's a letter for you. Hey, Nick!"

He looked up from his grapefruit, startled. Heather went to Point Reyes Station three times a week for mail, but this was the first time he'd received anything. Automatically, he reached for the envelope; then he saw the writing on it, and his hand jerked back. Marty had noticed. He saw it in her face, staring at him across Kathy's head, three tables away. He gritted his teeth and took the letter, then shoved it, unopened, into his pocket.

It was almost suppertime before he could bring himself to read it. He had gotten the new data caught up, but it had taken all day, and then there had been the batteries to recharge. After that there was no time to get to the Estero before Pembroke would have quit diving for the day. Nick's graphics program had developed a seemingly insoluble glitch, and he was sick of sitting at the card table in his hot, empty tent, anyway. He wished Dr. Anderson were back; Marty was still out with the girls; he needed someone to talk to. Aimless and miserable, Nick left his tent and wandered to the lookout. The heat hung over the camp like an electric blanket left on HIGH. People moved in slow motion, or mostly just sat, beer cans in hand, hardly even talking. Nick squinted out over the bay. No spouts. He shoved his hands into his pockets and found the letter.

He stared at the envelope for a long time; then, very fast, he tore open the flap. His eyes fled over the words, get-it-over-with quickly. Phrases leaped off the page at him; he sucked them in and tossed them out, not letting himself think.

Now you'll know what I did, encouraging you to apply . . . not an easy decision, but . . . I deceived

129

you, and I'm sorry, but ever since Richard died . . . terms with it, he's gone, you can't change it, or even—

And finally, "I thought, if you were forced to face it, you could say good-bye. It's not anger you need, Nick, it's forgiveness."

The letter was signed "Love, Dad."

Nick folded the letter into two, then four. Slowly, looking out to sea, he tore it into tiny pieces. There was no wind to catch the pieces when he threw them, only gravity. It seemed to take forever for them to disappear, swirling and floating like snowflakes, down to the bay.

"Look at the ants!" Junie exclaimed, just after breakfast on Saturday. She dropped her end of the suitcase Marty was helping to carry down to the van, and the heavy case banged into Marty's leg.

"Hey!" Marty said. She put the case down and rubbed her calf. She wanted to yell at Junie, and to stop herself, looked up at the sky. It was no help, too brilliantly blue, like the edge of a knife. The air was heavy with heat, stretched taut as a rubber band.

Junie was on her knees in the grass by a large anthill, watching a living black stream issuing from it. "There must be a million of them! Look, they're even taking their eggs. I wonder what's got them moving like that?"

Suddenly Marty was interested, too. "Something's scared them, maybe?" she suggested.

"It's like those gophers we saw yesterday. They were even crazier, though. They acted drunk. Remember how one of them kept chasing after Kathy?"

"Your mom's going to be chasing after you in a minute," Marty said, pointing to the parking lot, where Lyn was gesturing impatiently. "Come on, help me with that suitcase. What've you got in it, anyway, a dead body?"

"Books," Junie said shortly. She had her own ideas about family weekends spent touring wineries in the Napa Valley.

Climbing back up to camp after the Nivens had gone, Marty paused on the bridge over the little stream that emptied itself onto the beach. There was a strange, hot smell coming from the water. Frowning, she knelt to look at it. Bubbles were rising from the streambed. There weren't very many, just a few large, slow ones. Like jam cooking, she thought. Carefully, she touched the water with her finger. Yes, it was warmer than usual. Nowhere near boiling, though. Without knowing why, she licked her finger. It tasted the way the chemistry lab smelled in school.

Gophers acting drunk, ants abandoning their homes, streams going bubbly and bad tasting and warm. And that hot, elastic sky, too heavy, too still.

Danger, she thought, and it was like that other time, the time in the fog on the beach, running toward orcas.

Only they hadn't been orcas. They had been only Dr. Pembroke and Bill.

Suddenly and desperately, she wanted the whales. She straightened so fast she almost lost her balance, then bounded up the hill. She didn't see Nick watching her from his tent door as she tore through the camp, unzipped her tent door, and disappeared inside. In record time she was into the wet suit. Snorkel in hand, she dashed out of her tent again, single-mindedly heading for the trail to the beach.

But though she swam a long way out, and called them repeatedly with her mind and heard them singing, the whales did not come near.

The cod were streaming through the eelgrass, toothy with panic. In the kelp forest, golden stems dangled helplessly from their floats, holdfasts stirring in the mire below. Here and there, drifting, were luminescent blobs, disoriented by the greenish light. Deep-sea fishes, all bone and bulbous eyes, darted and bubbled in terror: *Where are we, where, where are, where?* A dolphin fled by, carrying its dead and rotting infant on its back. *Offshore, open ocean, away.* Somewhere, high pitched, came the wail of humpbacks.

The calf slept through it all. Its skin was translucent, the blood visibly throbbing. The veins were too near the surface, the mother observed, her eyes bathed in brine. The calf was losing weight, not gaining. And it tired so quickly. A short swim only, a joyous romp for a bare moment or two, and then, weariness, head pressed close to the mother's belly, nuzzling, needy. Every time it happened, the mother's glands responded with a prickle and a rush, and the milk poured out and out until the water all about turned creamy, but if the calf drank, it showed nothing of it on its body.

Nearby, swimming for the surface, was one of those not-alive-not-dead things that had made the mother think of orcas. *Men*, she reminded herself; they called themselves *men*, even swimming with unalive skin under the water and breathing air that was not there. Their minds still sang, though; she would call them man-singers. This one had not seen her yet. He had before, though, too many times. He did not like seeing her and the calf. She had heard his song, and when he spoke to that other one in the log, the outside voice and the song were one.

"That regulator of yours still not right, Bill?"

"I'm working on it," the other outside voice said shortly.

Regulator? the mother thought. She tuned into the man-singer's mind and pictured something round, like a stone, only clear as water with marks behind and attached to those large things that helped them breathe underwater.

132

When she listened again, the outside voice of the man-singer in the water was saying, "I think we may have to go right into the Estero after all."

"As long as those bloody whales don't keep hanging around."

"Haven't seen them today, thank God. And Ann Duguay's gone to the San Diego conference, so we won't have to worry about her spotting them for a while, anyway."

"But when she comes back—"

"We'll worry about that when the time comes. Maybe we'll have found the treasure by then."

"I still don't like it, Ray. And I don't like *them*."

There was a note in his voice that made the mother move a little closer to the calf's side.

"Don't get any stupid ideas, Bill." Sharply. "You think the whales are trouble now, you just see what happens if you try to get rid of one. They're *protected*, get me?"

Silence then, except for their songs. The mother lay still in the water, a fin hovering protectively over her calf. All around, the water bubbled, small bubbles, nothing like what might be coming, but all the same tasting wrong and sharp and hot. And still the deep-water scaled ones dashed their mad lines through the shallows, eyes wide with unreasoning terror; and still the silt at the bottom of the bay shifted and burbled.

So much to fear, the mother thought. So many reasons to go. She looked at the calf, so small, so quiet beside her. She could not go without it, and it could not go at all.

And there was, after all, a Song to be sung. A repetition that needed a singer. She was sure of it now.

Stranded by Song, she thought.

The calf sighed in its sleep, and the mother's fin stroked it, and there was no fear at all in her touch, only love.

CHAPTER THIRTEEN

SUNDAY WAS ANOTHER SEARING DAY. Marty didn't bother with breakfast, making do with a glass of iced coffee while helping Paul with the dishes. There weren't very many. A lot of the scientists were at the San Diego conference, and most of the rest had, like Sam and Lynda, taken the weekend off. Dr. Anderson was working, though. He had made an early start of it, trying to catch up on the data collection slowed by the bad weather earlier in the week. Nick had gone with him to help, though it was officially Nick's day off.

Washing the dishes, Paul didn't say very much, and Marty was glad. She liked him, especially the way he whistled or sang to himself when other people would have made small talk. He had never once asked her what grade she was in, or what she wanted to be when she grew up. He was the kind of person she might have talked to about the odd way the animals were behaving lately. But she was too tired. She had slept badly the night before, dreaming of black streams of ants and white-toothed orcas. Once she had sat bolt upright, staring into the darkness but seeing something else, a vivid picture of a strange boy. He had ragged brown hair and a wispy young man's beard. His skinny wrists stuck out of his shirtsleeves. His hands were tanned and callused, the fingernails very clean. He wore baggy pants that went only to his knees and patched knee socks below. He was on the deck of a small sailing ship, and he was alone. A cloud of birds blackened the sky overhead. Watching the boy from the water was a mother whale, her baby beside her.

Marty gave the coffeepot a last, unnecessary wipe. She could understand why she'd dreamed about the whales, especially after yesterday when the whales hadn't come near her. But that boy dressed in those old-fashioned clothes, his face so despairing and angry! Had she made him up? Certainly she had never seen him before. But he had seemed so real!

"That's the last of them," Paul said. "Thanks for your help, Marty."

She handed over the coffeepot, still thinking about the boy she had dreamed. Something about him reminded her of Nick. Not his looks—they weren't at all like Nick's. What, then? And what had that flock of birds meant, so big it practically covered the sky?

She wandered over to the lookout. On the *Leviathan* a couple of men were lowering the rubber dinghy into the water. Dr. Pembroke and Bill, it looked like. One of them climbed down the ladder into the dinghy. The other began passing down scuba gear. So they were going to be diving, and Nick wasn't here to watch them. Marty ran to get her backpack. She'd get to the Estero late, but Nick would think that was better than not going at all.

Unlike Dr. Anderson, Nick could never ignore the surf on the Pacific side of Point Reyes. At McClure's Beach, signs were posted on all the paths, warning of sneaker waves, sharks, and a notorious undertow. But more than the danger, it was the noise that appalled Nick. Even far back from the shore it was impossible to avoid it: an endless, rumbling roar like someone playing fortissimo on all the keys at the bottom of an organ at once. Sea birds made the high notes, sharp as the thrust of a knife.

Usually a buffeting Pacific wind added to the din. But today the heat lay taut and heavy on land and sea. Only the water could move under it, and even the water moved only at the shore. Farther out, the sea was a mirror for the birds that dotted the sky like braille.

"I'm heading for that outcropping of mica schist," Dr. Anderson shouted to Nick as he pointed to the south. On McClure's Beach people always shouted. "You take the granitic slope on the other side. It's our last fault zone here, and I'd like to get finished today."

Nick signaled to show he had understood. By the time he had picked up the surveying pole and other instruments, Dr. Anderson was a long way ahead. He walked the way he talked, pausing for nothing, moving on ahead, fast. He had worked both Nick and himself like a demon today. He didn't seem to mind the heat, but Nick was tired. He was tired of being hot, and tired of working. Most of all, he was tired of thinking.

What happened next, Nick was never sure. One minute he had Dr. Anderson in his sight near the top of the schist, and the next the older man was gone and a huge tule elk had taken his place. Briefly Nick stood stunned. Then he dropped the equipment and began to run. The elk bounded away before he got there, but there was no sign of Dr. Anderson. Nick had to round the outcropping before he could see the man's limp body, leg twisted at an unnatural angle, lying head downward only a short distance above the roaring surf.

The slope was treacherous, slippery with spray and loose pebbles. Nick took it on his hands and knees, edging down sideways, angling his course to bring him to the other man's outstretched arm. It seemed to take forever. By the time he was within touching distance, he was soaked to the skin and shaking. It had been hard enough to get down. How was he to get back up again with an unconscious man to carry?

He took the hurt man's wrist and shook it. "Dr. Anderson. Dr. Anderson!" He didn't know how loudly he yelled it.

"There's nothing wrong with my ears," said the other, harsh with control, "and I'd appreciate it if you left that wrist alone."

Nick put the wrist down very carefully. "Is it broken?" That was bad, but better than dealing with an unconscious man.

"Sprained, I think," Dr. Anderson said. He turned his head, slowly and painfully, so that he could look at Nick. "It's my leg that's broken."

Nick pressed his lips together, then nodded. "I can try carrying you."

"I think not. Not here. Can you get around to my other side?"

Nick didn't waste time answering. He crawled backward up the slope, made a skidding turn, and angled back down again. Dr. Anderson had turned his head the other way now, and was watching. He lifted his arm and placed it around Nick's lower back. "Good thing you're so skinny," he said. "Now, pull."

"With a broken leg, you want me to—?"

"I said pull! For God's sake, Nick, the tide's coming in!"

Sweating and straining, Nick began to haul the older man up the outcropping. It took a long time. When they were safe on the other side above the high-tide mark, Nick had to take deep breaths to stop himself from being sick. They lay there for some time, not speaking. Dr. Anderson's tanned face had a greenish look. His eyes were closed, two deep furrows between the brows. Clearly he could go no farther, certainly not the two-mile hike to the car.

"I'm going to get help," Nick said when he could manage a confident, clear voice. "You'll be safe here from the tide, and you need to rest. I'll be back as soon as I can. Where are the car keys?"

Dr. Anderson opened his eyes. "Pants pocket," he said. "Thank heavens I buttoned it, or they'd be in the bottom of the sea by now. Damn that elk! I thought there wasn't anything left that could make me jump."

Nick took the keys and got to his feet. "You old enough to drive?" Dr. Anderson asked, trying to smile.

"If I wasn't before," Nick said, "I am now."

Marty lifted her head. There was Estero sand in her nostrils, under her tongue, even between her teeth. She was hot, and her skin prickled, and her head felt muzzy with sleep. Bleary eyed, she squinted between clumps of beach grass to the dazzling waters of the Estero. Yes, the red-and-white dinghy was still out there. Maybe she hadn't been asleep for very long after all. But the position of the dinghy's anchor rope had changed. The mud flats were narrower, too. A quick glance at her watch confirmed her fear. She had slept for hours.

The last time she had looked at the dinghy, Bill had been in it, working on a lot of bulky equipment. Now the equipment was gone, and so was Bill. A small patch of water just off the channel was ruffled up, and the harbor seals nearby were shifting about anxiously. So that was where Pembroke and Bill were. She couldn't see Bill's snorkel tip or Pembroke's scuba bubbles from here, but she was as sure of it as if she could. They hadn't gotten very far in their search, she thought, remembering where they had begun, just to the north of the channel. Either they were being very thorough, or they had come upon something promising. Maybe she'd missed them bringing up some treasure. Nick would never forgive her if she had. She wished she hadn't fallen asleep.

Whenever she inhaled, she had to close her throat to keep from choking on the grit in her mouth. Carefully, she spat out what she could. It still seemed very hard to breathe. Drowning in sand, she thought, and shivered. Her mind opened like a crack of light at the back of a dark cave, and she saw a ship's hull lift itself at an impossible angle out of the Estero. How had it done that? And then, from the cracked planks of that hull, a boy hurtled into churning water. Down, down, no time to breathe, cold, oh, cold, rough, where am I, surface, have to breathe, have to—and then the sea was pouring into his open mouth, only it wasn't just sea, it was mud, too, a lot of mud, and—

The crack in her mind slammed shut. Drowning. Oh, God. Drowning. Her hand scrabbled at dune grass, and her eyes were closed.

"I don't think we're ever going to find that bloody wreck."

Bill Lancaster's voice. Marty opened her eyes. She was lying here in the beach grasses beside the Estero, and the sun was shining hot and hard, and there was no one drowning, no one at all. She saw Bill standing at the water's edge, helping Ray Pembroke take off his tanks. How had the two men surfaced without her noticing?

"You sound as if you don't believe the frigate is here at all," Dr. Pembroke said over his shoulder.

"I believe Drake brought it here. You wouldn't be doing this if he hadn't. But how you know he left it here—"

"It was a coastal frigate, very small. It could never manage the Pacific, where Drake was going. And it didn't go north because Drake had taken it north once already, and the conditions there turned them back. And it wouldn't have gone south, because the Spanish were there, ready to rip into them for all the things Drake had done. For God's sake, Bill, how many times do we have to go over this? The Tello frigate *must* have stayed here."

"What if somebody else read the archives the way

139

you did? What if they found the wreck here first, and robbed it?"

"There'd have been some record of the sale of the treasure. Ming porcelain is too rare not to—"

"All right, Ray, you're the expert. I just go along for the ride."

"And the money," Pembroke said softly.

"Haven't seen any of that yet, have we?"

"The artifacts we've found so far are worth something."

"Half of whatever we get is mine," Bill said. "That was the deal. Fifty percent."

"I know the deal," Pembroke said coldly.

"There's enough light to keep diving," Bill replied. "I'm willing if you are."

"I think we need a break. Let's get back to the *Leviathan*. We're beginning to get on each other's nerves."

Nick was closest to the Bear Valley Visitors' Center, so he went there. All the time he was telling the rangers what had happened and phoning for an ambulance and letting Heather know, he felt in control, even efficient. It was when everything had been done and he had to sit on a bench and wait for the stretcher party to be organized that the sickness returned. He kept remembering how close Dr. Anderson's head had been to the water; the stories about great white sharks riding in on waves to take bites out of seals sunning on the beach; the feel of the heat squeezing the sweat out of him all the way up that interminable slope; the sounds of a strong man trying with everything he had not to groan, and failing.

When people were in enough pain, they died. It was a fact. You couldn't ignore it. Scientists talked about how different people had different "pain thresholds"; doorways into pain was what they meant. Nick had thought about it a lot. He knew pain already *was* a threshold. It was the edge between life and death. It was a wide edge, but the only way to get to the end was by going through it. People had said Richard hadn't felt a thing. Nick knew that they were wrong.

"Here, son," a ranger said, handing him a cup of hot, sweet tea. "You look like you need this."

Where there was no pain, there could be no danger. Nick took the tea and drank it. When he was finished he stared numbly into the sugary mud remaining at the bottom. Keep away from the edge; don't let yourself feel anything; keep yourself to yourself; no reaching out. It was a good rule. He'd been following it pretty well—until Point Reyes.

"Where is he?" a voice demanded brusquely.

Nick lifted his head. It was Pembroke. His penetrating eyes stared endlessly into Nick's, willing him to speak. Nick pressed his lips together and didn't reply. "I said, Where's Jonas? Where did you leave him? Is he conscious?"

Still Nick said nothing. The ranger who had given Nick the tea led Pembroke a short distance away, saying, "The boy's had a hard time, Dr. Pembroke. A bit shocked—the tea he's drunk'll help—but you can't expect people to react normally after something like this. He'll be all right by the time the stretcher party's ready."

"I've seen shock before," Pembroke said. "The eyes go all vacant, not like that kid's. He's not talking because he doesn't want to talk, it's as simple as that."

Pembroke had gotten that right, Nick thought. It disturbed him that the man had been able to read him so easily.

Pembroke was still talking. "Has he said where he left Dr. Anderson?"

"Yes, quite accurately. It's a distance from the McClure's Beach trailhead, but we've had to do this kind of thing before. You wouldn't believe the trouble park visitors can get into. We know what to do."

141

"So we can find Dr. Anderson without the boy? He doesn't need to come along?"

"No, but he'll want to. It'd be better for him to see your friend safe than remembering—"

"He's better off going back to the camp with Miss Kent, and having a good long rest in his tent. Where is she? Oh, there you are, Heather. Listen, while I go with the stretcher party, I want you to drive Nick back to camp."

Resentment flared in Nick. He got to his feet and marched over to them. "I'm going with the stretcher party."

"Listen to Ray, Nick," Heather said, putting her hand on his arm. "You look worn out. There's no need—"

"No."

"But—"

"*No!*"

"He won't be able to sleep until he's sure Dr. Anderson's out of danger," the ranger said, and Nick sent him a grateful glance before looking defiantly at Pembroke. Pembroke's eyes were expressionless, like bull-kelp floats, Nick thought with distaste. How could Richard have liked this man?

"He might as well come, Ray," Heather said. "He can sleep in tomorrow. Jonas won't be piling the work on Nick for a good long while."

"If Jonas's leg is broken badly enough," Pembroke replied coolly, "Nick might just find himself on his way back to Vancouver. Jonas can't justify keeping on a computer technician who hasn't got any data to compute."

Back to Vancouver. Back to Dad. No chance of showing the world what Pembroke was. Leaving Marty with the whales.

Leaving Marty.

"I know how to collect the data," Nick said.

"Ah, but do you know where?"

Nick was silent. Pembroke was right. Dr. Anderson had always had to tell Nick what rocks to measure, and what columns to record the data in. But Pembroke didn't have to sound smug about it. Why was he so pleased at the idea of Nick's having to leave Point Reyes? One thing was certain. Whether Pembroke had guessed about Nick's connection to Richard or not, he didn't like Nick any more than Nick liked him.

"There's that stretcher," Pembroke said. "Sure you don't want to go back to camp, Nick?"

Somehow Nick kept the knot of sickness in his stomach from showing in his face. He shook his head.

"So you're the type to stick with silly decisions," Pembroke said. "Personally, I believe in flexibility. You get so many more opportunities that way."

CHAPTER FOURTEEN

IT WAS PAST MIDNIGHT, BUT HOT, MUCH too hot to sleep. Marty had been trying all that Sunday night to make a pencil drawing of the baby whale. Just before the Coleman lantern went out, she put her pencil down and stared at the drawing. She was good in art, and the drawing was right, at least in form, but it simply wouldn't come to life. There was no joy in it. Slowly, she crumpled the paper up, feeling oddly sick.

A long time ago she had heard the Nivens come home from Napa. Junie and Kathy were having one of their arguments, so Marty stayed in her tent. Nick came back about an hour afterward. Marty knew because someone greeted him by name, and later a shocked voice said, "But is he okay, Nick?"

Was who okay? Marty almost went out to see, but it would have looked funny, after avoiding the Nivens. Besides, she still felt guilty about falling asleep at the Estero today. She had overheard a lot, but there was still no proof that Pembroke and Bill were doing anything illegal. If she had kept herself awake she might have seen something worth photographing—maybe the two men holding one of the artifacts they had talked about. Instead, she had nothing to report to Nick except that he was right about them treasure hunting.

In her darkened tent, she peered out the east window, trying to see the moon. After a few minutes she located it, low on the horizon, just beyond the Nivens' big tent.

144

It was a half moon tonight, and it had an odd reddish tinge. Last Monday night it had been full and round and so brilliant that swimming under it had been like being bathed in the white light of a giant lantern.

It had been six nights since she had swum with the whales. She wanted them. She wanted them so badly the insides of her elbows ached. First there had been the bad weather, and then Junie and Kathy had gotten sick; and then, the one chance she had been given she had wasted daydreaming. After that they hadn't come, though she knew they were still nearby.

She let her fingertips slide down the cool, slippery wall of the tent. The mother whale's skin was like that, only colder and alive and amazingly soft, except where it was mounded with barnacles. The calf had hardly any barnacles. Despite its length it was easy to think of it as a baby. There was something untouched about it, an innocent quality to the way it had played with her: rough tumbles until the mother intervened, and then quiet and big-eyed trust. Marty turned uneasily away from her window. A human baby would have nursed and slept after all that activity. The calf had not fed on anything the whole time she was with them.

The wet suit was where she kept it, stretched out by her sleeping bag like an empty body always keeping her company. Almost without thinking, Marty dusted herself with talc, then wriggled into it. *Never dive alone.* Well, she wasn't going to dive, she was just going to swim. And anyway, if the whales came, she wouldn't be alone. As for waves, ever since Friday the sea had been calm, leveled by the heavy heat. Nothing to worry about there.

Outside, the night was a flat, charged weight of darkness. Marty stood for a moment with her back to her tent. With her flashlight off she could see only the tents to the east, outlined against the sky by the dim russet moonlight. They seemed very small and precarious; every-

145

thing did under that sky. The stars were incredibly bright, but did nothing to lighten the blackness. It was like being at the bottom of a deep, dark well. Marty almost had to force herself to stand erect. For the first time in her life she was aware of the enormous vertical column of air above her. Pressure, she thought. The same, only less, that whales would feel when they dived very deep.

She turned on her flashlight then and made her way through the camp and down the trail to the parking lot. There was no wind, not even a breeze. Every sound was magnified. Marty could hear snuffles and whines and the snap of twigs near the lake to her left as clearly as if they were right beside her. Wings flapped above her head. Far away at the edge of hearing a dog barked endlessly, over and over, and always the same pattern; *bark, bark, bark-bark-bark; bark, bark, bark-bark-bark*. It got on Marty's nerves. The sound faded as she got closer to the water, but it never quite stopped.

At the beach, the surf was virtually nonexistent, a swish and a trickle, that was all. Marty stood at the very edge of the pale water, seeing the moonlight in it and listening for spouts. She heard only her own breathing. Her hair lifted from her neck. Was the wind coming up? She put her hand toward her hair, and it met her halfway, full of static and crackling. In the insulated wet suit, in that hot, hot night, Marty shivered. And then the whales were there, and she forgot everything else.

She splashed into the water: ankles, knees, thighs, chest; she was swimming; the water was cold and held her up and her hair floated like seaweed. The whales were a long way out. They knew she was there, and the tide was in; there was no reason for them not to come closer. Her feet beat the water, one-two-one-two, inefficient without flippers, but somehow taking her a long way. Yet the whales were farther still, and the mother wanted to dive, she wanted to go right away from here, she wanted to head for Chimney Rock and the west and the deep Pacific beyond. *Don't go!* Marty cried to her, or the calf did; their songs blended, they were the same. *Don't leave me!*

And the mother, despairingly agreeing, *I cannot. I will not. What will be has already been sung. My calf and I can do nothing. But you, female man-singer, your melody is new. I fear you for that. And you seek to cross boundaries that should not be violated. I will not swim with you.*

Marty's feet were cold. Her hands were cold, and her face. Her hair dragged at her. There was a pain in her chest, deep, deep; she gasped for air to push the pain away, but somehow the air wouldn't come. Come, oh, cold, rough, where am I, surface, have to breathe, have to—

And then the mother whale was there, her flipper under Marty's body, lifting her, lifting, and there was air to breathe, and it did not feel like a weight anymore. And Marty breathed and breathed and then slid down the great length of the mother's flipper and lay against her side, breathing air the mother gave her and weeping hot tears into that cold, wet, pulsing skin so insulated that it could not feel them. And the great flukes beat up and down, up and down, shoreward. It did not seem far at all. When it was too shallow for the whale to swim any farther, Marty let go of the flipper and the soft, cold side, and swam ashore, and she didn't look back, not even once.

Before dawn on Monday Nick was up and dressed and pacing in his tent. It had always been crowded in the tent, with the card table and computer and the two camp beds and all the suitcases. With Dr. Anderson gone, it seemed much too empty. The stretcher party had made reasonably fast work of getting the injured man off the schist and back up to the van. From there it had taken only a little more than an hour to get him to the hospital. But then there had been a long, long wait, first for the doctor, then X rays, then all the usual red tape in admitting Dr.

147

Anderson to a room, and, finally, some treatment. A nurse had to give him a shot for the pain before they could set the broken leg.

"What will you want me to do while you're in here?" Nick asked him afterward.

"You've got enough data with today's stuff and yesterday's to keep going for a few days," Dr. Anderson replied. "And there was that graphics program you were working on. Got that glitch out yet?"

"Almost."

"So you've got a week's work left, anyway, and it won't hurt you to have a couple of days off after that. I won't be in shape to go climbing around rocks for a while even then, but I'm bound to be out of here. You can do my climbing for me until my cast is off. Can't he, Ray?"

"We'll see what the doctor says," Pembroke said.

Nick saw the look he exchanged with the doctor, and later, when the nurses kicked them out, he stopped one of them determinedly and asked how long Dr. Anderson would be in the hospital.

"At least six weeks," the nurse said cheerfully, "and probably more like eight. He needs traction, you see. Good thing he has insurance."

Six weeks, Nick thought miserably, following Heather down the hall. It was practically the middle of July now. By the time Dr. Anderson was out of the hospital the summer would be over. And Pembroke would make sure Nick would be out of a job long before that.

Nick wondered if Marty knew. She had been in her tent when they got back to camp last night. The Coleman lamp was on, so he knew she was awake. He had wandered that way a couple of times, and once had gotten as far as the tie backs of her door, but then Lynda Niven had called him over and started asking him questions about Dr. Anderson and he hadn't had the nerve to try again. He should have, though. He ought to have found out if Marty had seen Pembroke at the Estero yesterday. And she should be told about Dr. Anderson. She should know about Nick maybe having to go back home to Vancouver early. And with those two kids around her all day today, he wouldn't have a chance to talk to her alone until tonight at least.

The sun was up. She was bound to have slept enough. With sudden decision he unzipped his door.

It was only just after six, but already the day had the dry, scratchy, electrically charged feeling of towels that had spent too long in the dryer. There was no dew. As he slipped across the clearing to Marty's tent, Nick was startled to see a line of jackrabbits, ten at least, cross his path. They were heading for the dining tent, of all places. What on earth were they doing? He paused, watching them. The dining tent was zipped tight, but the first jackrabbit didn't pause. It bounded right into the dry canvas as if to make its own way through, bounced off, and tried again. The others waited patiently. After two more tries, the leader seemed to know it was stymied, and the whole line of them hopped off down the hill toward the parking lot.

"That," Nick muttered aloud, "was one of the craziest things I've ever seen."

He continued on his way. No one else in the camp was up. When he got to Marty's door, he paused. The flap was open, only the screen door zipped up. Inside, it was shadowy and quiet. He made a face. You couldn't knock on a tent. "Marty?" he whispered. "Marty, are you awake?"

There was a movement inside, a swish like silk. Then she was at the door, holding a beach towel in front of her that almost hid the thin, pale nightgown behind. Her hair was disheveled, her dark eyes wide and strained looking. Only the screen door was between them.

"Nick," she said, low and soft. It made something

149

strange happen to his stomach, hearing her say it like that, and looking the way she did.

"I need to talk to you."

"I'll get dressed," she said.

He turned his back. Her bare feet padded away, accents in a swish of silk. Silence, then another ripple and swish. He pictured her pulling the nightgown over her head. Long hair catching on lace; skin paler than the nightgown; darker places where her body would make its own shadows. Movements, arms over the head, graceful fingers pleating the silk and dropping it to the floor, feet stepping daintily out of its crumpled circle . . . He closed his eyes, but it didn't help; the scene unrolled in his mind like a projector that couldn't be turned off. Now she would be getting dressed. He heard the sound of denim being pulled up, first one long leg, then the other. The quick shake of hair over a top. No time to have put on a bra.

He was breathing too fast. He had to get control of himself. She'd be out here in a minute. He made himself take a deep breath, keeping his shoulders rigid and low.

She unzipped the screen door. "We'll go for a walk," she said.

He nodded, not looking at her. With one accord they headed for the tarmac trail. "We could get to the Estero and back before breakfast," Nick managed after a minute. He risked a quick look at her. He had been right about the bra. Her peach-colored tank top was no tighter than anything she ever wore, but there was a difference today, a hint of hardness under the soft fabric, a swing. His stomach tightened. He was breathing too fast again.

"Beach path or bluffs?" she asked, when they were at the Visitors' Center.

"Bluffs."

He followed her up the steep path. Her jeans were old and fit her perfectly. Her legs were very long and slender. She wasn't even winded when she reached the top.

She turned to him then. "What's wrong?" She was looking at him with those enormous, unblinking, dark eyes, catching him unawares. He stared back, feeling as if he were drowning.

"Not here," he got out at last. "I want to walk."

He took off, very fast. She almost had to run to catch up. It was then, half jogging along those crumbling bluffs with streams of birds flying overhead in a sky stretched tight as elastic, that he told her. "And if Pembroke has his way, I'll be out of here by the end of the week," he finished. "No way of proving what he's up to. No job. And my father—" He broke off. He had told her about his father once already, that night when the whales had pushed him to shore.

"A week may be enough," Marty replied slowly. She had been silent the whole time he spoke. Now she told him what Pembroke and Bill had said at the Estero the day before. "I'm sorry I didn't get any pictures."

"A photo wouldn't have proved very much. The important thing is, he's narrowed down the frigate's location to the Estero. That's not so big, really, not compared to the whole of Drake's Bay. And I'll have more time to watch him now. You may be right, Marty. A week just may be enough."

He looked at her, swinging along beside him, eyes trained straight ahead. There were deep shadows under them, and her skin was unnaturally pale. "I'm sorry if I woke you too soon," he asked awkwardly.

"It wasn't that early. I just—went to bed late."

"Couldn't you fall asleep?" She didn't answer. Suddenly he knew why. He stopped walking, caught her by the shoulder, and pulled her around to face him. "You went swimming with those damn whales again, didn't you?"

Her chin went up, but the corners of her mouth were trembling. "What do you mean, again?"

"Don't play games. I saw you last Monday night. Hours, you swam with them. And you did it again last night, didn't you? You put on Lynda Niven's wet suit and you went out by yourself in the dark into some of the most dangerous waters in the world when the first rule of diving and even swimming is never to do it alone. Of all the stupid stunts—"

"So I'm stupid!" she flared. "Who cares? Anyway, nothing happened. I didn't get killed. I—" She broke off suddenly, shook her head furiously, and started again. "Anyway, I wasn't swimming alone. The whales were—"

"Those whales! They're just animals! What do they know about people and their needs? Say you got caught in a kelp bed. They wouldn't know how often you need to breathe. They wouldn't give a damn, even if they did know. You'd drown and they wouldn't do one thing to save you. And what about great white sharks? This place is crawling with them. Put those whales and you in with just one of them—or even an orca—and they'd be gone. You couldn't keep up with them, and they wouldn't care. It's crazy, Marty, you swimming with them like that. It's—unnatural!"

She looked down, biting her lower lip. The trembling had spread to her chin now. Her hair was a coppery nimbus around her face. He loved it, even with her standing there full of misery, he loved it. His fingers longed to touch it, but it was too foreign, too far away, an elusive beauty, out of bounds. And she stood there, untouchable in her grief, and he wanted to touch her, he wanted to reach her, to understand her, he wanted to know all about her: what movies she liked; who composed her favorite music; what she thought about when she listened so quietly to other people talking. Other things, too. There would be places where her skin would be even softer than where he'd already touched; there'd be places where it was whiter. She would turn her head just so, if he touched her in the right way. Without the tank top her hair would tumble over her shoulders, burned-caramel silk over white silk; without the jeans there would be more whiteness, long, strong legs fluid against his. "Annie's Song" all over again, only to Nick's beat. Curves and lines mingling, two into one, all the hot aches he felt drowned in her darkness.

A sudden fury possessed him. Why did she have to care about the whales? Harshly, he said, "You don't mean anything to those two whales, Marty! Nobody means anything to them. They don't care about people. We're just curiosities to them."

She shook her head violently. "I almost drowned last night," she said. "They saved me. They saved you, when you were lost in the fog. Why would they do that if—?"

"Why do animals do anything? Why do people? There doesn't have to be any *reason*. Just instinct, hormones, whatever you want to call it. It's like this"—he kissed her lips, sudden and savage and not at all knowing he was going to do it—"and this"—less savage this time, lingering. She went very still, motionless as a doe in headlights, making no sound. He was frightened by her stillness. His mouth opened to say something, but he forgot to draw back, forgot what he was going to say, forgot everything but the feel of her lips. He could taste her tears, tangy as the sea. "Don't cry," he muttered against her mouth. "Marty, don't—"

His hand trailed a slow path downward from her chin; her skin was the silky nightgown he had imagined her taking off. His other hand dropped from her shoulder, his arm going around her, pulling her toward him, encircling her. She leaned against his chest, slender and still and beautiful, and she wasn't crying anymore, and her lips were moving under his. Gentle, gentle, oh, Marty, oh! and opening, and his tongue, and hers, heart turned drum, and touching, here, and here, and—oh! here.

153

And the sun beat down out of that cloudless, powerful sky, and jellyfish went ashore by the thousands onto the mud flats of the Estero, where clams already lay dying, and the channel fish bared their teeth at one another and stopped swimming, and bull kelp tore itself from its holdfasts and drifted away. And through it all, offshore, two whales lay quiet, waiting for a chorus to be sung.

CHAPTER FIFTEEN

 "MARTY? ARE YOU ALL RIGHT? MARTY?"

She couldn't look at him. She ran her fingers through her hair, pulled ineffectually at her tank top, bent over, and straightened the hem of her jeans.

"You're so beautiful," Nick whispered.

Her voice was sad. "Do you say that every time?"

"What do you mean?"

"You don't carry a—those things—around in your wallet for nothing."

He reached for her, but she twisted away. After a long moment he said, "No, I don't say it every time. I said it to you because I wanted to, because it's true." She turned her head. "Marty, please don't."

"I've never—" She swallowed, then took a deep breath. "I didn't know anything. And you—"

"All right," he said. He grasped her chin, forcing her to look at him. "There've been other girls, the kind you do things with because it's what you both expect and there's this hammering deep down inside and you just stop thinking sometimes. But when it's over, it's over. They try to act as if they've given you a great big valuable part of themselves and they haven't; they even know they haven't. And you haven't given them anything, either, and you know it, too. That's what's wrong with it, see? But with you—oh, Marty, it was beautiful. It was the most incredible—"

She stared at him, her eyes enormous, and briefly the

155

truth of what he was saying overrode her fear and her shame. Yes, it had been beautiful. Like high music, up and up, soaring and painful and joyous, no need for words, cycling higher and achingly higher until there was nothing else but her own need and Nick's and her giving to him and he to her and all that generosity bounding and rebounding like a repeated echo that grows instead of dying away. She had forgotten who she was, then. She had stopped being the Marty who was only a baby-sitter and barely passing in school. She had even stopped being the Marty who had turned to the whales because they understood her without needing her to be what ordinary people thought was useful. With Nick she had become someone else altogether, someone immensely valuable, with a value that was much more than just physical. It depended on what she was, not what other people wanted her to be, and it had made for a meeting of astonishing power and joy.

And yet she was also that other Marty who was only a baby-sitter. She was the Marty who had been refused by the whales. She was the Marty who would probably have to drop out of school because she could barely talk, let alone read. And there was Nick with his blue eyes and wide-shouldered, lean body and his big brain and experience. After this summer he would be in college. He'd have nothing in common with her. Even if he didn't start thinking she was the kind of girl who did this all the time, she would remember what he had said about all those other girls, and maybe she would forget that he had said they didn't matter. One by one the doubts and uncertainties layered themselves on the truth of what had happened, and it was like whalesong with all its confusing harmonies and complexities. She wanted to find a bed of eelgrass and twine and wind it about herself and lose herself in it, she wanted to be still, she wanted things not to have happened.

But she couldn't look away from him.

"Marty, listen to me. I didn't want this to happen, either. I tried and tried not to fall in—"

Shrill cries interrupted him. Two small bodies were charging along the bluffs toward them. "Marty! We've been looking everywhere for you!" Junie and Kathy.

Marty stepped back at the same moment that Nick dropped her chin. Junie arrived first. "Marty, it's ten o'clock. You were supposed to start taking care of us at nine." She frowned puzzledly at Nick, then turned again to Marty. "It's okay, though. We told Mom you were just in the washrooms. She and Dad have gone to Bolinas."

Kathy panted up then. "Why weren't you there, Marty?"

"I'm sorry," she got out, her hand reaching automatically to stroke the little girl's hair. "I—lost track of time."

"Don't blame Marty," Nick said gruffly. "It was my fault. I needed to talk to her. Something private."

Junie's eyebrows rose, and she looked thoughtfully from him to Marty and back again, but she didn't say anything. Nick muttered, "I've got to get back to the computer. See you." He gave Marty a long, urgent look, and then strode off.

"So what's with you two?" Junie asked, when he was out of hearing. Marty said nothing. Junie squared her shoulders, seeming much older than her age. "None of my business, huh?"

"Marty," Kathy said, tugging on her arm. "We want to go to the Estero again. Can we? Please?"

"The birds have all flown away from the Visitors' Center," Junie put in. "Even the swallows have left. I want to see if they've gone from the Estero, too."

"*I* want to see the pirate anchor," Kathy said.

Junie said exasperatedly, "I've told you and told you, it's not really a—"

Some things never changed. Marty took one last look backward along the bluffs. Nick was growing smaller and

157

smaller. "We can look at birds and at the anchor both," she said aloud, the baby-sitter again, while deep, deep inside her, something dived, looking for eelgrass.

The calf would not feed, but it would still swim, when the mother urged it. It rarely dived, though. And so the two whales swam on the surface, a slow, sleepy, up-and-down of the flukes, calf paced, going nowhere. Round and round, back and forth, essential because today the mother could not lie still, aimless because the only destination she wanted was out of reach and impossible, anyway, denied by Song.

They were swimming outward from the breakers when the white-and-red log came. As soon as the mother heard its roaring, she prepared to dive, singing a note of warning to the calf. But the calf paid her no heed, continuing its trancelike, surface swim. *Calfling!* Her voice was wild, full of overtones. It should have summoned the calf. It would have, if only that log had not been making so much noise. It was nearer now. The calf swam on, directly into its path, unseeing, unhearing.

The mother was afraid of few things, and none of them for herself. Now she was afraid. She sank under the surface until only her blowholes were in the air, and swam quickly to the calf's side. There were two of the man-singers in the log. She could see them with the blurred bending of vision that comes at the boundary of water and air. She thought one of them was pointing at the calf. She thought the other picked up something from the bottom of the log. She thought the thing was long and rigid and sticklike except at its end, which was shaped like the tip of a fluke. She thought of the terrible sharpness of shark teeth.

No, you will not, man-singer, that you will not!

She breached, fast, slamming her vast body down upon

158

the water. In the enormous turbulence that followed, the calf submerged, whether swamped or of its own will she couldn't see. She herself was winded and startled at the pain in her belly. She lay bobbing in her own waves, one eye searching for her calf, the other watching the log as it tossed from side to side. The roaring noise it made had stopped. That was something, at least. But it ought to have turned over. It must be more balanced than it appeared. The man-singer who had pointed to the calf had fallen flat, but the other was keeping himself upright by holding tight to the edge of the log. He still grasped the sharp stick. Anxiously, the mother lifted her body vertically half out of the water, her flukes moving the great head in a complete circle. Where was the calf?

There! Surfacing close to the log, much too close, its blow surely audible even to off-balance man-singers. *Not there, calfling. Away!*

But even as she sang to it, she could hear its fear and confusion. She knew it did not know where to go. And when a calf does not know where to go, it seeks its mother. She called again, a single, high, keening note, the same one over and over. *Follow!* She couldn't wait to see if the calf obeyed; already the waves were dying away, and the log was tossing less wildly. She dropped flat from the vertical and began to swim out to sea. A few heartbeats later, she stopped and turned around underwater. There was no sign of the calf. She searched for it with echoes, and in her mind she found it: a small, living, familiar thing, right beside the unalive echo returning from the man-singers' log.

The calf did not know where she was. It had not listened to her when she called. It had forgotten how to use its own Song's echoes. It lay in a still, breathless panic on the surface of the water, and it did not move.

Back the mother swam, fast, fast, sounding at the end and coming up between the calf and the log. The man with the stick was pointing it at the calf. The mother reared herself upright, shoving the calf aside with her flukes. There was a sound like thunder, followed immediately by a hiss. The mother's head jerked backward. Against her tongue, inside, she could feel the tip of something hard and shark-sharp.

"You fool, Bill! You goddam fool!"

"You said you were worried about them. You said—"

"They're protected. And they're intelligent. It's—oh, what's the use? Anybody stupid enough to use a spear gun on an adult gray—"

"I was aiming at the calf! How was I to know the mother would come up like that?"

"Get that motor going. This is big trouble. I mean it! Move!"

None of this meant anything. The mother noted it, added it to the Song, and still it meant nothing. There was no pain. She would not allow there to be any pain. A metallic stream poured into her mouth and out through her baleen, dyeing the water red. She shook her head violently, trying to free herself of the sharpened stick. But it was stuck fast, and she had no teeth to break and chew it, the way the orcas would, or the sharks. Sharks. They would be smelling her blood already. Soon they would be here. And she with the log still to deal with, and those man-singers in it. Maybe they had more of those stick-things. And the calf still lay there. No way to protect it. It must be protected. It must. The calf saw her desperation and tasted it and the water was red and the log roared suddenly and then choked and sputtered and went silent and all at once the calf was doing what it ought to have done a long time ago.

It was swimming away, frenzy fast.

"The calf's heading for the Estero!"

"It'll strand itself. And the mother'll go after it. And then *she'll* strand. Two stranded whales, one of them

160

speared. We'll have the whole goddam world down there watching. We can bloody well kiss that treasure good-bye. To say nothing of police. They'll trace the spear gun, you can be sure of that. How're you going to like going to jail, Bill?"

"We'll have to get the spear back."

"From a live adult gray?"

"She might not be alive. Anyway, if she's stranded, what can she do to us? It's not like she has teeth."

"You make me vomit, Bill."

Man-singing, nothing but man-singing. And meanwhile the calf was heading toward the one place in the world it must not go. With a spear in her cheek the mother abandoned the log and swam after her calf, trailing a long, bubbling stream of red behind her. And behind that, with a creak of oars long unused, came the dinghy from the *Leviathan*.

They were about halfway to the Estero when Junie noticed the boat. Marty hadn't seen it. She was staring straight ahead, not out to sea, and she hardly heard a word of what the girls were saying. But the word *Leviathan* caught her, and she turned her head quickly. Now that she was paying attention, it was easy to identify the sound of Dr. Pembroke's dinghy and the familiar colors. "Heading for the Estero, I'll bet," Junie said. "That's Dr. Pembroke steering. I wonder if they're going to use the magnetometer ag— Hey! What's that other guy doing?"

Marty stopped dead. Whalesong burst into her mind. *Calfling!*

"There's a whale out there," Kathy said excitedly. "See, it's a little one, right over—" Her voice changed. "Marty, the boat's going to bump into it!"

"No, it's not," Junie said. "See, Pembroke's turning to

get out of the way. But that other guy's got a spear gun. You don't think—?"

Whalesong, loud, so loud! *No, you will not, man-singer, that you will not!*

"Look!" Kathy yelped.

Out of the water rocketed something unimaginably vast, a living torpedo of mottled gray, gigantic mouth wide with streaming baleen. For a single breathless moment the entire body was in the air. Then it landed. *Slam!* Waves exploded around it. A ringed fountain of spray flew into the air. Marty clapped her hands to her ears, but the crashing chords of whalesong were in her mind, not her ears; she couldn't shut them out. She was breathing hard, as if it were she who had thrown forty tons of her own weight as hard as she could onto the surface of the water. With a kind of double vision, she watched the dinghy rock violently. The engine had conked out. Pembroke was flat on his face, but not Bill. He was hanging on to the lifeline, and the spear gun was in his hand.

"Go away, Calfling. Please go, please." Marty didn't know she was speaking aloud.

A long pause. The calf remained motionless. There was now no sign of the mother whale, not even any whalesong. The water was calming down. The mother *must* be visible, if she were still there. Which meant she had dived, hoping the calf would follow. The calf was without protection. And in the boat—

"He's going to shoot the baby!" Junie shrieked.

Pembroke had dragged himself to his knees. Even from here it was possible to see his desperation, straining toward Bill, trying to knock the spear gun out of his hands. The calf lay still.

Hiss. Thunk. *Pain. There must not be pain.* But there was pain. Marty cried out with it, whalesong, words, it didn't matter, it was all the same, it couldn't be more

162

different. *I didn't, we didn't, don't blame, oh, don't die, oh, talk to me, even if you won't swim with me, please—*

She might not have existed. The calf, galvanized by shock, was bolting through the water, heading directly for the channel that led into Drake's Estero. The mother was trying unsuccessfully to rid herself of the spear in her cheek. Marty caught images, bare threads of Song, the calf, orcas, teeth, rage at the man-singers, the calf again, blood-stink in the water, sharks. Nothing for her. Nothing for Marty at all.

And now the dinghy was rowing after the whales.

Marty turned to the two girls. "Get help! Go!" She was screaming it, not saying it; her hair stuck out from her chalk white face. She was like something out of a legend, something not quite human. A small part of her knew she was frightening them, but it was only a small part.

"You mean, me, too, Mar—" Kathy began, but Marty was already gone, hurtling along the bluffs toward the Estero. Junie threw a hunted look at the dinghy and then she, too, started running, but in the opposite direction, back to camp. Kathy hesitated. She couldn't run as fast as Junie. And she could still see the baby whale. She could see the mother, and the blood trail she was leaving, and the boat that was rowing slowly and steadily after it.

Then Kathy began, as fast as her stubby legs could carry her, to follow Marty.

CHAPTER SIXTEEN

NICK GOT ALMOST AS FAR AS THE DESCENT to the Visitors' Center before he stopped. He could see the camp on the bluff opposite, but not the valley in between. It was as if there were only one bluff here, not two. He stood still, looking at the small, pale speck that was his own tent, and his spirit rebelled. I can't do it, he thought. I can't sit down at the computer as if nothing's happened, when Marty and I have just—

He hadn't meant it to happen. The things about her that attracted him were the very things that kept him at a distance. Coming to Point Reyes, he hadn't wanted to talk to anyone about anything, yet somehow he kept talking to her. And it wasn't just about the weather, or even flirting, which would have been bad enough. He told her things that he didn't want anyone in the world to know, things he hadn't even realized he knew himself. She made it happen by listening, listening with all of her being, not thinking about what her hair looked like or whether she had taco sauce on the corner of her mouth or what smart thing she was going to say when he finished. She just listened. A still center, he thought, thinking of a poem he had read somewhere; *his* still center. How could you not revolve around your own center? The thought was profoundly disturbing. He sat down in the wild grasses at the top of the bluff, and hugged his knees to his chest, and kept on thinking.

Her isolation. That had attracted him, too, so like what

he wanted for himself that he ought to have respected it. But he hadn't; he hadn't even wanted to. Instead, he had done what he would have loathed someone else doing to him, he had watched her in secret: watched her learning to snorkel; watched her in the dining tent and biking off with Kathy and Junie; watched her stare out to sea, longing for the whales; watched her swim with them and be free with them. As if she somehow thought she had more in common with whales than with humans!

It was a laughable idea, if only she could see it. Slim, fragile Marty having anything in common with a whale! Maybe there were people you could imagine being a little like whales, but Marty wasn't one of them. What you needed was someone big and strong and self-confident and smart, someone with no natural enemies, someone you couldn't imagine ever dying except maybe of sickness or old age. Never young. Never in accidents. Because accidents shouldn't happen to smart people; their brains should keep them alert to danger and out of trouble. That was like whales, too. Whenever Nick read about whales stranding themselves in shallow water and dying there and rotting on the beach, he felt, mingled with his pity, a deep sense of betrayal. Whales were smart, they should know where it was safe and where it wasn't, they should stay away from the edges, where trouble boiled up like surf in a storm. If the biggest-brained creature on the face of the earth couldn't keep itself safe, how could anybody?

In the end those two whales would rejoin their own kind. They were alien creatures, living in an alien environment. No matter how much Marty loved them, they would go away and leave her. She would have been better off not letting herself love them at all.

He hadn't wanted to let himself love Marty. He hadn't wanted to need her. He hadn't wanted to give her anything of himself. He had just wanted to keep himself to himself, whole and safe. But this morning he had forgotten that

that was what he wanted, and he had loved her, and needed her, and given her so much of what he was he didn't think there was anything left to give. And then he had found out that he was wrong, there was more to him, and more and more, vistas opening within himself that he hadn't even known were there, gentleness and generosity and unself-consciousness along with an alien world of excitement, of being more alive than he could have believed possible. Pushing what it was to be human right to its limits.

He rested his head on his knees. He couldn't remember ever being so tired. He felt as if he had walked an enormous stretch of cliff, razor thin and with a precipice on either side and no end in sight. He'd only paused here; the journey wasn't over. He couldn't even pretend to himself that he could go back. He was on the edge, and he'd stay there, dangerous though it was, moving on ahead, struggling to stay balanced. Two into one, he thought, and hugged his knees tight in sudden terrified exhilaration. What he had felt this morning was something he would never cease wanting, again and for always.

Pounding footsteps jerked him out of his thoughts. He looked up to see Junie. She was all by herself and there were tears on her face. She had been with Marty. Now she was alone, and she was crying. Marty! He leaped to his feet. "Junie, what's—?"

"They shot the mother whale! She's not dead, not yet, but they're going after her into the Estero, and the baby's there, too, and I'm supposed to get help and I don't know how—who—" She was sobbing openly now.

He took hold of her shoulders and shook her. "Marty— where is she? Is she all right?"

"I don't know! She's going to the Estero to stop them! But she hasn't got any weapons—and—there're two of them, and they're grown-ups and they've got spear guns and I'm scared, Nick, and I don't know where Kathy is and—"

"Was it Pembroke?" Nick interrupted grimly.

She nodded through her tears. "It wasn't him who shot the mother whale, though. He even tried to stop the other guy from doing it. But what's he gonna do now? It's against the law to shoot whales. That guy was in his boat. It was his gun. Pembroke doesn't know there's anybody who can prove he tried to stop it. Maybe he'll think he has to finish the whale off, or at least get rid of the evidence. And Marty won't let him near her. You don't know Marty. She won't—"

He did know Marty. Junie was right. She would do everything in her power to stop Pembroke and Bill from getting near the wounded mother whale again. "You go to the rangers at the Visitors' Center," Nick said, icy cold. "Tell them I've gone ahead to help. They'll know what to do."

He was running even as he said it.

Whalesong filled Marty's mind, tumultuous and stupefying, chords crashing on chords, a great and roaring dissonance. It was like being inside a cathedral organ, all the stops pulled out, flute and string lost in the deafening thunder of deepest bass. Edge smashing against edge, forever destructive. Pounding down the path that led to the Estero, Marty cowered into herself, trying to escape the clamor; but she was in it, it was in her, part of it was even for her.

For us there can be no meeting. Our Songs are too different. We are two species, not one. We are opposed.

Marty didn't even try to answer. Two species, not one. It was the truth. She couldn't hide from it like a whale in eelgrass. She was not of the People. She was of the species that for centuries had sought out and killed the People for oil, or meat, or sport, or for ambergris to make perfume, or for the whalebone in ladies' corsets. She was of the species that had no end to its wants, the species that believed it had no limits and so crossed over them time and again.

But everyone had limits. And not all the limits were bad.

It was an odd place for the truth of it to come to her, there on that steep descent, slipping and sliding and grasping at bushes to keep from flying off the cliff into the stony shallows below. Limits didn't have to be bad. Even her own limits didn't have to be bad. She couldn't read very well and she found it hard to say the things that were in her mind. But she could speak to the whales. She could sing with them and hear their songs. She could hear the one Song and know herself to be a part of it. Maybe she wouldn't have been able to do these things if she had been really good with words.

The path was rounding the cliff corner; she was going too fast. She grabbed for a bush growing sideways out of the hillside, skidded, and half fell. Lying there, twisted sideways to hold on to the bush, the Estero spread out below her, Marty saw the calf stranded on a mud flat and the mother surface-swimming toward it. Marty tried to get up, but there was something wrong with her ankle. She tried again, somehow managing to get to her knees. Up, she told herself. One leg started to obey her. Not the other. She wasn't paying enough attention, that was the problem; she was watching the scene below her; she wasn't working hard enough. Deep breaths. That was it. Up. *Up.* The mother whale was swimming more slowly, trying for caution. But the Estero was shallow, and the tide was dead low. All the caution in the world wouldn't stop her from stranding if she swam much farther in. In the channel, Marty saw the boat from the *Leviathan*. They were rowing it. No motor. That was why she hadn't noticed it coming in.

"Marty? Marty?"

A small hand was plucking at her elbow. Serious eyes stared into hers. "Kathy! What're you doing here? I sent you back to camp!"

"You sent Junie, not me." Kathy's chin trembled. "Marty, the baby whale's stuck. What are we going to do?"

The mother whale was closer to the calf, so close the spear in her face actually brushed the mud the calf was lying on. The dinghy was inside the Estero now, heading directly for the two whales. There were things that must be done, Marty told herself, and tried once again to get herself upright. She couldn't. "Help me up, Kathy."

"Your ankle's all twisty."

"It doesn't matter. You'll be my crutch. We're almost down the path now, anyway."

"What if that man shoots the whale again? Or us?"

"We'll stop them," Marty said firmly.

"How?"

"Never mind how. You just put your shoulder under my arm—it'll be hard, because I'm going to lean on you. Ready?"

Kathy ignored her, leaning forward to look down at the Estero. "The boat's anchoring! And—oh, Marty!—that man's getting out another spear!"

Another spear. Marty took hold of Kathy's shoulder and hauled her back. "I said, are you ready?"

White showed all the way around Kathy's eyes. "Ready," she said.

And then they both stood up.

Nick had never run so fast in his life. Sweat poured down his neck and into his eyes; there was a stitch in his side; the muscles in his legs burned. He was almost at the descent to the Estero—too far back from the edge to see most of the water, only just the far Limantour shore, empty. No black specks of seals. No birds. No life anywhere, in a place that ordinarily teemed with it. Nick noticed only in passing. His eyes were desperately searching for whales, and a boat with two men in it, and Marty. He could see nothing of any of them, either.

They must be almost directly below the precipice, closer to the cove. He wouldn't see them until he got right to the edge. He jammed his elbows hard into his sides and charged on. Almost there. A few more paces. Slow down, or you'll fall. That's better. Control, that was the thing, and balance—half speed, leaving plenty of space to stop. Funny how the ground got to feel when you were tired. Spongy, sort of, as if it wasn't quite secure, when it was really you who were—better stop now. Don't want to tumble over the edge.

Nick stopped running. He stopped walking. He stood still. He knew he stood still, yet he could feel movement under his feet. Muscle wobbles, he told himself scornfully. He was out of shape. He dropped to his knees, he didn't know why, then flattened himself against the ground. He felt both his hands clutching clumps of grass. The movement under his body continued unabated. It was like lying on a giant Jell-O mold. Nick's heart pounded. Okay. This was California. Everybody knew there were earthquakes in California. Nothing to worry about. Just another one of those thousands of peaks on the seismograph down in Bear Valley. Let go the grass, Nick. You've got to get to the edge of the cliff where you can see.

He couldn't make himself release both hands at once.

One hand went first, reaching quickly for another clump of grass as he squirmed forward, then letting the other flash out and latch on to the thick stem of a giant cow parsnip. He knew he was being stupid. Handholds were unnecessary in a small earthquake, and they were useless if it was going to be a big one. A big earthquake uprooted everything, making mile-deep crevices in the ground as the two tectonic plates slammed together edge against edge, shattering cliffs and sending tsunami waves roaring in to swallow up the land and change the shape of things forever.

He was close to the edge of the bluffs now. The whole of the Estero was spread out before him. He could see the dinghy from the *Leviathan*. It was anchored in water that changed every moment: now rolling one way, now another, sometimes flattening as if under a great weight or dropping almost to the muddy bottom or rising like a mountain chain with peaks that looked like knives. Pembroke was lying in the bottom of the tossing, rolling dinghy. He was wriggling—could it actually be calmly?—into the only pair of scuba tanks in the boat. Bill was half sitting, half lying, holding on to the lifeline with one strong hand, the loaded spear gun in the other.

Not at all far from the dinghy was the calf, motionless on an undulating mudbank. Nick could see nothing of the mother whale's body, and knew she must have dived. He hoped it was somewhere deep, but with the Estero the way it was, nowhere was reliably deep for long. If she stranded, too, he didn't know what Marty would do.

Marty.

He had looked for her everywhere but where she was. Somehow he had expected her to be with the whales or at least nearer the water. Where he finally discovered her was dangling from the cow fence that edged the foot of the cliff near the trees. She was hanging with her back to the wooden gate of the cow fence, using only her upper

171

arms to support her weight, and she was being shaken up and down with each quake, and the gate was splintering all around her. A little girl—Kathy—was holding on to one of Marty's knees, whether to steady herself or trying to help Marty, Nick couldn't make out. He was across the cove from them and had the whole long path down to descend once he got around: a fair distance under normal circumstances, let alone in an earthquake.

He made himself let go of the cow parsnip and began to pull back from the edge of the bluffs. It wasn't so bad, really, just very quivery, no sign of any uprooting, let alone crevices. And it was dying away, he was almost sure of it. His stomach felt much less shaky than before. The earthquake was almost over.

But still the sun blazed in an aureole of unnatural colors, and still there was so much static that Nick crackled as he moved. He found himself holding his breath. In the unnatural silence he almost thought he could hear something. The sound was high pitched, too high for Nick to be certain he was hearing it at all. But he could see the calf writhe on its mudbank.

Whales have better hearing than we do, he thought.

He stopped thinking then. He had to. Because with a noise like a Learjet coming in for a landing, the world went suddenly mad.

CHAPTER SEVENTEEN

ALL THAT HAD COME BEFORE WAS AS nothing compared to this. Great sheets of light flashed across the sky. The earth heaved out clay and mud and stones like broken bones. Meters-high jets of water fountained upward. Whole acres of land sank, bluffs snapping off and crashing into the sea, rocks turned shrapnel, bursting apart. The noise was stupendous, a grinding, shrieking, earsplitting pandemonium. Marty couldn't block it out, and she couldn't bear it; she knew she was screaming and couldn't even hear herself doing it. Helpless as a rag doll, she was tossed from the gate, landing on the jolting earth almost on top of Kathy. They clutched each other, two wide-eyed, open-mouthed, terrified faces pressed together, and it was like being in the engine of an express train with the whistle on full and the throttle jammed open, roaring and racketing over track bumpy as dinosaur vertebrae, and no handholds anywhere, nothing to clasp but each other. The cow fence behind them tore itself in two, and a solid section of gate collapsed on top of them. They were grateful for it, after the hurt, because it protected them a little from the stones hurtling down the bluffs. Somehow Marty worked herself and Kathy farther underneath its wooden shelter and got a hand between one of the boards to hold it where it was. The shaking went on and on, up and down, heaving and buckling, a land turned liquid beneath them.

It stopped finally, not all at once, but so gradually that

173

they almost didn't realize it was over. Marty knew it when she could hear Kathy's scream, thin as a bleat in the growing silence. "Shh," she whispered, "hush, Kathy, shh." Slowly, Kathy quietened. The silence grew profound. Marty lay still, listening to it, knowing it to be unnatural. The earthquake wasn't over. There was more, much more, to come.

Somehow she pried her hand from their makeshift roof. Her fingers felt numb; she had to use her other hand to open them. Somehow she got herself and Kathy out from underneath. The ground was motionless, but she felt as out of balance as a sailor after a long sea journey. She tried to get to her feet and couldn't. Her ankle wouldn't obey her. It didn't hurt, but it wouldn't work. "Are you all right, Kathy?" she said.

"I'm bleeding. I need a Band-Aid, right here. And my head hurts where the wood hit me." She took Marty's hand and placed it on the top of her head.

"A real goose egg," Marty said. "Anything else? Can you stand up?"

"Acourse I can." She got to her feet. "It's easy now the ground's staying still. Want me to be your crutch again?"

"Good idea. And hey, get me that broken plank over there, will you?"

Calm voiced, that was the way, no need for Kathy to be scared again before she had to be. Between the piece of wood and the little girl Marty got herself to a standing position. She tested her foot on the ground. Her ankle gave way when she put any real weight on it, but she could limp. There was still no pain. Funny. No, wrong word, there was nothing funny here, nothing at all. More earthquake on its way, and Kathy to be looked after, and her with a sprained ankle that wouldn't let her move fast, and all kinds of decisions to be made and acted on in who knew how little time. The bluffs around the cove looked completely different, sharp edged where large chunks had

174

broken off and tumbled down. Were things up there solid now, or would more rocks come down in a second big quake? Should she and Kathy stay here, where they had already shown they could survive, or would they be safer higher up? Inland would be best, but could they get that far in time? Could they even get higher up, with the cliffs so changed?

"Let's take a good look around," Marty said, still very calm.

Their backs were to the Estero, so the first thing they noticed was that the part of the fence that had not collapsed had moved a long way backward to the foot of the bluffs. There, where once a snowy egret had fished in a quiet pond, six fence poles stood drunkenly, leaning barbed-wire loops over something that was no longer a pond or even a pool. All the water had disappeared. Now there was only mud, with gaping clams and starfish and dying fish writhing on it, and the sodden ribs of an ancient shipwreck sticking out from the detritus. Marty looked at the wreck and wondered, but there was no time now for anything but survival. She eyed the cliffs that surrounded what had once been the pond, and saw with relief that there was still a path, though it had changed. Now it had a steeper bottom, and in one place it hung out over the hull of the wreck like a shoulder just waiting to shrug. So that was one question answered. They could get up the path, if her ankle held, as long as they did it at once, before the earthquake got started again.

Into the eerie silence came whalesong, a deep, low moan. Almost with shame Marty turned her back on the cliff path and looked out into the Estero. It was an unfamiliar place, the waters emptying out of it even as she stared, a maelstrom swirling out to sea like bathwater down a huge drain. Fast, deep, overflowing the banks of the channel, swamping all the sandbars, it flowed, and still it flowed, a constant outpouring, noiseless as death;

175

nothing to hear, not even a gurgle, except for the constant dirge of whalesong.

The water leaves, and I grow heavy, and my calfling's Song is done. And, oh, the weight of it, the weight!

It was hard to make out the body of the mother. Mud colored, she blended into the silt at the bottom of the Estero, one mound among many, only the spear standing out as foreign. The calf was easier to see because it was higher, stranded already before the Estero had begun to empty. It lay very still and did not sing. Could not sing. Could never sing again.

. . . the weight of it, the weight!

Marty wept. She didn't look at the dinghy from the *Leviathan*, overturned in the mud, or at Ray Pembroke taking off his scuba tanks and unclipping himself from the anchor line and standing up in the mud and somehow scrambling ashore. She didn't look for Bill or wonder where he had gone. She could only stand and cry, and Kathy took her hand and cried, too, and the impending danger did not matter, the passing time did not matter, nothing mattered, because a baby whale was dead.

And, oh, the weight of it, the weight!

Nick was halfway down the broken path to the Estero before he managed to get a good view of the wreckage the earthquake had wrought there. Despite the fact that he was on his feet and forging stubbornly ahead as soon as the worst of the shaking began to die down, it had taken a long time for him to get here. He had to detour around all the new raw cuts in the clifftop, going long distances inland before he could find places where they could be crossed. Sometimes the land he put his full weight on sank like the crust on a pie, so that he had to test every step or end up prying himself free. Nick could only be grateful for the sparse vegetation on the bluffs; he couldn't imagine trying to fight his way through tree roots and branches as well as everything else.

When he finally saw what had happened in the Estero, he caught his breath in shock. The water was almost entirely gone. Here and there were tiny pools or outward-flowing rivulets, but the rest, easily three miles of water from the nothernmost tip of Schooner Bay to the sandbar at Drake's, was gone. A waste of mud and wet sand remained, glinting with the bodies of dead fish. Nick shook his head in awe. The force of that earthquake, to make such a change! Had the land risen so much above sea level? If it hadn't—"

He saw Marty then. He hardly recognized her. She was covered with mud, even her hair weighed down with it, and she was some distance out in what had once been deep water, a little north of the cove. There was a huge hill of mud beside her. He saw both of her arms, small as two twigs, outstretched to grasp something sticking out of that hill. She jerked backward, lost her balance, recovered, took a tighter grip of the thing sticking out of the hill, and jerked backward again. Nick knew then what it was. The hill was the mother whale, and Marty was trying to remove the spear.

He started downward at once, trying to watch Marty and keep his footing on the treacherous path at the same time. It wasn't easy. He fell twice before Kathy appeared, a tiny muddy blob, beside Marty. If it hadn't been for her bright orange sand bucket that still matched a few clean patches of her backpack, Nick wouldn't have seen her at all. She poured water from the bucket onto the mother whale's body, while Marty still tugged on the spear. Then she turned and waded away through the mud, aiming for one of the tiny pools of water that still remained on the Estero bottom.

Trying to keep the mother whale alive with a sand bucket and a couple of weak arms! It was one of the most

177

gallant things Nick had ever seen, and one of the most futile. Two girls, all alone with a giant gray whale stranded half a mile from the ocean, trying to deal with a spear gun and sunburned whale skin while little by little forty tons of the whale's weight settled downward, crushing its own organs, destroying itself.

Why had it gone into the Estero at all? Okay, its calf had panicked and gone in there first; okay, any mother would have wanted to help. But she must have known she would only strand herself too. Cut your losses—it was the smart thing to do. She obviously hadn't been able to help. Almost certainly the baby was dead. Nick could see its body on what had once been a sandbar, and he could see its stillness and the way Marty and Kathy were ignoring it. So it was dead, and the mother was stranded, a brain as big as some cars, and what was the point if you didn't listen to what it told you?

Nick stumbled on a rock and angrily recovered. The whales would have known there was an earthquake coming, they'd have known it long ago. They would have heard the vibrations that humans couldn't; they were smart enough to put two and two together. They should have gone away into the deepest offshore waters, where they would have been safe. Instead, they had gone into the Estero, the worst of all places. And now the baby was dead, and the mother lay there, destroying herself by her own bigness, her own carelessness, her own lack of foresight. All for nothing, all her own fault!

And Marty still wanted to save that whale. He shook his head furiously, and there was water on his cheeks. To keep himself from thinking where it had come from, he made himself look for Pembroke and Bill.

Had they been swept out into Drake's Bay with the receding Estero waters? Nick shaded his eyes with his hands and stared out to sea, but there was no sign of any boat. The ocean was curiously flat, as if something were pressing on it. There were jagged colors around the sun, too. Nick hurried on. He didn't like the look of things. There might be aftershocks. He had to get Marty and Kathy out of here.

At the place where the newly sharpened cliff jutted out into the path, he lost sight of the girls, but what was left of the cove was now revealed. The rubber dinghy was in it, upside down. Nick nodded to himself. He remembered now that they had anchored the dinghy there. It had overturned, but the anchor had stopped it from being swept out to sea with the receding Estero waters. Where were Pembroke and Bill? A flash of white caught Nick's eyes, something two legged and two armed clambering up a mud-filled slit that had once been the stream draining the pond at the foot of the cliffs. It was Pembroke.

He was wearing swimming trunks and a long-sleeved, many-pocketed white shirt that clung to him wetly but appeared amazingly clean against that backdrop of endless mud. He had a huge coil of thin Alpine rope over one shoulder, and something that looked like a crowbar in one of his hands. Only from the knees down was he filthy. He was past the stream opening now, at the beginning of the pond area. But it was a pond no longer. Nick had expected that. What he hadn't expected, what jumped out at him and made his breath catch in his throat, was the ancient ship's hull that now stood partially revealed near a deep crack in the silt of the pond bottom.

The wreck was incomplete, several of the ribs missing, as were most of the long planks that had covered them. There was a broken-off pole sticking up out of the mud, almost halfway down the hull. Was that what was left of the mast? Had the little ship been damaged in a storm and somehow made its way into the sheltered Estero only to founder here in the pond? But this would have been deep water centuries ago, before the deforested land eroded and silted it all up. It would have been protected, too,

179

with the cliffs surrounding it. Why should any ship have foundered, once it had actually managed to make its way in?

Oddly enough, the wreck was still balanced on its keel, though that was deeply buried in the pond bottom. Its bow was buried, too, but the stern was just visible, sticking about an arm's length out of the mud. Built to stand up higher than the bow, Nick reasoned, like Spanish galleons he had seen on old movies on TV. But this was much too small to be a galleon. It was no more than three meters wide, and ten to twelve at most in length.

Frigate size, Nick thought.

His gaze leaped back to Pembroke. Alpine rope. A crowbar. Nick breathed hard. A smile formed itself on his face. So Pembroke, too, thought he had found the wreck he had been searching for for so long.

Nick's eyes glittered. He got down on his hands and knees to keep Pembroke from seeing him if he should happen to look up. Then he began crawling down the path, aiming for the place where the right side of the cliff face had fallen away, leaving the path practically overhanging the wreck. He would get a good view from there. He cursed the fact that he hadn't brought a camera. But maybe Pembroke would find some treasure. Maybe he'd actually take it away. And then Nick could tell the proper authorities that he'd seen Pembroke take it from a national park, and they could search Pembroke's belongings and find it. It would be as good a proof of Pembroke's crookedness as a camera. Maybe even better.

Nick was at the overhang now. He flattened himself to the path and slowly, slowly, let himself peer over the edge. Pembroke was actually on the wreck, the crowbar between his knees, frantically scooping mud away from the decking with his bare hands. The floorboards looked solid enough, where they were visible. Probably built of teak, a good, hard wood, rot resistant. And there were muds whose

180

chemical consistency slowed decomposition. Pembroke stopped snooping suddenly, swore, and nursed one of his hands as if he'd struck it on something hard. There were only a few yards between Nick and the wreck, and Pembroke's curses were easily audible. After a minute he went back to clearing the mud away, but more carefully this time. Nick watched, his own heart beating faster. Something was coming out of the mud, something barrel-shaped at one end and tubular at the other. There was a crusted loop at the top. It was a cannon.

The other man was muttering to himself. "The right shape, by all the gods, and Tello's century. What bloody marvelous luck!"

A long, silent pause. Pembroke turned his back on Nick and dropped the coil of rope onto the mud inside the wreck, keeping hold of only one end. Now his body was in the way. Nick couldn't see the cannon or anything else. He could have yelled with impatience, but he held his breath instead, listening hard. He was rewarded by Pembroke's muttering again.

"That ought to do it," he heard. "Don't want to lose the location, if that water—"

The rest was lost in a grunt as he began hurriedly scooping out mud again. His shirt was white only in patches now. After a long time he took the crowbar from between his knees and began to pry away at the decking he had cleared. Pembroke was trying to get into the hold.

Once he started using the crowbar, it was easy to see what he had done with the rope. One of its ends was now made fast to the cannon loop. Nick frowned, puzzled. Why had he done that? The other end was still loose, lying with the coil on the mud, so obviously Pembroke wasn't intending to haul the cannon up by the rope, at least not right away. And anyway, he couldn't, not a heavy cannon, not all on his own. That made Nick think of Bill again. Where was he, anyway? Just before the big earthquake hit, Nick had seen him in the boat, holding on tight to the lifeline while Pembroke squirmed into scuba tanks. Only a single set of tanks on board, and Pembroke the one to wear them. And now Pembroke was down there right this minute, alive and cursing, and Bill Lancaster was nowhere to be seen.

Nick thought of a man holding on to a puny lifeline with a single hand. He thought of an overturned boat. He thought of the power that must have been in all those tons and tons of water, pouring out of the Estero into the sea. And no scuba tanks on the man. Even with scuba tanks it would be hard to survive the whirlpool tug that water would exert, miles and miles of it trying to get through that single narrow channel like bathwater down an unplugged tub. Without tanks, how could anyone have survived?

Nick hadn't known Bill Lancaster very well, and what he had known he hadn't much liked. And Junie had been quite clear that it was Bill who had shot the mother whale. All the same, Nick felt sick, thinking of what had almost certainly become of him.

There was a sudden triumphant yelp from below. What had Pembroke found? Nick leaned out to see. The older man was lying flat on the muddy deck, straining one arm deep inside a hole he had made. "If that isn't porcelain," Pembroke said almost prayerfully to himself, "I'm Sir Francis Drake."

Nick must have made a sound. Either that, or some instinct made Pembroke look up. For a long instant they stared into each other's eyes. Neither moved. Then Pembroke withdrew his arm, slowly and carefully, bringing it out of the hole in the decking empty-handed. At the same moment Nick lifted his chin and said, "So this is what you've been looking for all summer."

CHAPTER EIGHTEEN

THERE WAS A LONG PAUSE. PEMBROKE was obviously thinking hard. But when he spoke, his voice was smooth and unconcerned. "Come down here, will you? I think we have things to talk about. And it's silly saying them with you flat on your stomach and me with a crick in my neck."

Nick hesitated. Then he shrugged. Pembroke was right, it was silly. He got to his feet, scrambled down the rest of the slope, and waded through the mud toward the wreck. Marty, he reminded himself. But with Marty the whales always came first. She must know how worried Nick would be about her after the earthquake. She should have been worried about him, too, at least enough to go back to camp and look for him! But instead she stayed out there in the Estero with a whale that was going to die, anyway. Putting the whale ahead of him, even ahead of her own and Kathy's safety. So let him put something else ahead of her for a change.

"There's a solid rock ledge over there under the mud," Pembroke said, sitting up and pointing to a spot on the far side of the wreck. "Keep away from that crevice, though. The edges are still falling in."

Nick wished he hadn't said what he had about Pembroke looking for the wreck. It showed he had been watching him, and it showed he was suspicious. What he should have done was play innocent and hope Pembroke would make a mistake. But maybe it wasn't too late. Nick nodded his thanks at Pembroke and slogged through the mud to the place he had indicated. There was solid footing with a thin layer of silt on it exactly where Pembroke said.

"You took me by surprise back then," Pembroke said in a friendly way. "What I've been looking for all summer is contaminated soil and water—heavy metal pollution, actually. Nothing to do with this wreck. Finding it was just sheer luck."

Nick said, "I knew that. I don't know why I said that other thing. The earthquake shook me a little, I guess."

He hadn't meant it as a joke, but the other man grinned. "You and everyone else."

Nick was physically drained, still shocked by the terror of the earthquake, and Marty was out there in a waterless Estero with a six-year-old kid, and there might be more quakes coming, and even if she hadn't thought very much about him, he still wanted her safe. And people were *dead*. Pembroke's own partner was dead. A man who could grin at an unintentional pun in such circumstances was an easy man to hate, even without any other reasons.

Pembroke didn't seem to notice Nick's silence. "I wasn't sure for a while there whether I was dead or alive. But it's an ill wind, as they say. When I climbed up here I found this old wreck. Who wouldn't check it out?"

"A lot of people wouldn't," Nick heard himself saying, "not when there's been a quake that's caused so much damage, not when they don't know what's happened back at their own camp, not when their partners have been swept out to sea and killed. A lot of people would think the last thing that matters is an old wreck."

Pembroke's lips tightened. "Now you listen to me. I'm sorry as hell about Bill Lancaster, but there wasn't and isn't a single good goddam thing I could do for him. I barely survived myself, and only because I thought of clamping my tank harness to the anchor line. Without tanks, in the seas that were running in here when that quake hit, Bill wouldn't have had a chance."

"Why did *you* have tanks, and not him?"

Pembroke made an impatient movement. "He should have had them. His regulator wasn't working, and he didn't bother fixing it. We were diving in shallow water, so he said it didn't matter. I told him and told him—" He broke off. "Look, I don't have to explain anything to you. And anyway, there may not be time. There's bound to be aftershocks with a quake like that. The wreck may be buried again. And I think there may be some cargo in her."

Nick said nothing. Pembroke's voice speeded up. "Nothing valuable, mind you, except to the archaeologists, but it'd be a pity to lose whatever it is, especially if it's historically important."

"You're going to give it all to the historians, then," Nick said as calmly as he could. Pembroke's arm was creeping back into the hole in the decking. Nick watched it in fascination. Did the man even know he was doing it?

Pembroke spoke faster still. "Drake left a ship in his Nova Albion harbor, see—a frigate, like this one. Took her from a Spaniard named Rodrigo Tello off Costa Rica, and it sailed with the *Hind* up the coast to Nova Albion, where Drake abandoned it. If we could get all the cargo out of this wreck, and there was something there that the historians could prove was on the Tello frigate, that'd be proof positive that Nova Albion was here in Point Reyes. It's something the scholars have been arguing over for years, Drake's anchorage in California. We could earn a place in the history books with this one, Nick."

The story was all too plausible. If Pembroke really did turn everything over to the archaeologists, he might get people patting him on the back instead of putting him in jail, where he belonged. And all Nick's watching and waiting, all his *knowing* that Pembroke was a phony, all of it would be worthless. He imagined Pembroke smiling

185

on TV, explaining how he had reasoned it all out, how he'd risked his life to prove it; and all of it such good publicity for Conservocean, the dollars pouring in . . .

Nick took a deep breath. He couldn't allow it to happen. Pembroke must be caught, somehow. But he couldn't think of anything that would catch him. Pembroke knew things and took advantage of what he knew with a flashing cleverness that Nick's brain had to race to catch. He was an opportunist, and Nick was not. It was that simple.

"The thing is," Pembroke went on persuasively, "we don't want to lose any of the cargo to an aftershock. And I'm just one person. So what do you say to giving me a hand getting it all out while there's still time? Call it a job interview, why don't we? I'll be needing an extra hand on board the *Leviathan*, now that Bill's—and anyway, you could use the job, with Jonas out of commission."

Nick didn't dare look at him, for fear of what Pembroke would see. The way he was using Bill's death and Dr. Anderson's accident to try to get what he wanted out of Nick! Nick had a strong feeling he wasn't going to win any battle of wits with this man. He wasn't, maybe, going to win any battle with him at all.

"So will you work for me, or not?" Pembroke said, impatient at Nick's long silence.

Nick threw caution to the winds. "People who work for you seem to have short life spans," he said.

This brought Pembroke up short. "You're talking about Bill?"

"Bill, yes. And other people."

"Such as?" Pembroke's voice went suddenly soft.

Too late, Nick found reason. "Nobody in particular."

"Young. Nick Young. That's your full name, isn't it? I had a student named Young. Richard Young, he was. Twenty-two, built like a bear and just about as cocky, nothing could hurt him, not our Richard. Died in a bomb

186

blast last summer, very unfortunate, promising student like that. You're related to him, I suppose?"

Through his teeth Nick said, "My brother. As you obviously know."

"I figured there was a reason for you treating me like a pariah. Blame me for Richard dying, do you?"

"If he hadn't come to work for you—"

"Why did *you* come here? I'd have thought it'd be the last thing somebody like you would do. Hell, you wouldn't even go to Richard's funeral. You're an ostrich, not a confronter. So what are you here for?"

"I don't believe in funerals," Nick said, his voice trembling. "A lot of phonies pouring out compliments about somebody who isn't there. Not even all his dead body was there, Pembroke. I'll bet they were wiping up bits of him off your deck for months."

"That's my fault? Your brother was a fool, boy. Bright enough in his way, but a fool. He thought he was bloody immortal. I told him there had been a bomb threat. I told him not to sleep on board that night. He usually didn't when we were in harbor—a girl in every port, that was our Richard—but it was like everything else, he had to show he wasn't afraid. So he slept on board, and there was a bomb, and he was blown to smithereens. His fault, boy, not mine."

Nick bit his lip so hard it bled. He licked it, making himself notice the metallic flavor, counting as he inhaled, as he exhaled. Richard wouldn't choose to sleep on board that ship just because there had been a bomb threat. Maybe it was true that he was never afraid of the things he ought to be, but to do something like that . . . ! No, Nick didn't believe it. He cast around in his mind for something that would give the lie to what Pembroke had said. "If there was a bomb threat, why weren't the police there, watching?"

187

"The police have too much to do to post a guard every time somebody gets a vague bomb threat."

"If it was that vague, why'd you warn Richard at all? You told him it was vague, didn't you? That was why he didn't take it seriously. He knew—"

He broke off. There was a sudden silence. Pembroke's eyes were different, Nick thought. They reminded him of an animal, a raccoon, maybe, cornered while foraging for garbage. There was something here, something Pembroke didn't want probed. Either it hadn't been a vague threat, but a serious one, in which case the police ought to have been there, or it had been vague, and Pembroke shouldn't have bothered with it, either.

"Just because the police don't take things seriously doesn't mean I don't," Pembroke said, as if reading his mind. "I have a responsibility to my ship and my crew, after all. I take precautions against any threat, no matter how vague. Of course I would warn Richard." He shrugged. "I should have known better. Richard was a confronter, see? He did it everywhere, every time. He would never have gotten his Ph.D. There was no compromise in him, and he thought he knew best about everything. He got his teeth into causes and worried them to death. It made him a damn good protester, I'll say that for him. He could get into the thick of the action better than anybody I've ever met. Snooped his way in if he had to—"

He stopped abruptly. Nick controlled his rising rage. Pembroke had said more than he had intended, just now. That meant something. And the cornered look was back in his eyes. What did it mean? Why did Pembroke look like that now, when he talked about Richard snooping, and before, about the bomb threat? What was the connection?

Pembroke turned away. "I'm not going to waste any more of my time on this. If you don't want to help me, fine, but I'm going to get as many of the artifacts out of this boat as I can, before it's too late."

Nick moved forward, leaving the safety of the rock ledge. From the side of the wreck, he said very loudly, "My brother was not a snoop."

Pembroke ignored him, reaching a long way into the hold. Whatever he was feeling for obviously eluded him. He supported himself with one arm and leaned forward even farther, grunting with effort. His head disappeared into the hold, along with most of his upper body. Sounds came from within the ship, and Nick, watching, thought the hull moved a little in the mud. When Pembroke's face reappeared, he was so carefully not smiling that Nick looked immediately at his hand. There was nothing in it, but there was a noticeable bulge in his shirt pocket.

"Going to give that thing in your pocket to the historians, are you, Pembroke?" he jeered.

Pembroke's eyes went very green. Slowly, he reached into his pocket and took out a small, thin, bowl-shaped object. He wiped it on his sleeve, and what had been mud-colored and uninteresting turned into something translucent white, with blue markings.

"Ming dynasty," he said softly, "worth more than its weight in gold, though nobody knew it in Drake's time. That's why he left it here, of course. He was overloaded; he had to leave something. Men, mostly, they take up the most room, and they have to be fed. But he didn't like to be thought a monster; nobody does. Abandoning more than a dozen sailors in a wilderness like the West Coast of North America in those days—well, even Drake must have felt a little bad about it. So he had to tell them he'd come back; maybe he even had to believe it himself. Treasure, he'd have called the porcelain; he probably liked it well enough, too, though he must have known there was no market for it. It wasn't until 1700 that anybody in England wanted Chinese porcelain." All the while Pembroke was talking, he was polishing the little bowl lovingly.

"There's a lot more of it in there, isn't there?" Nick said. "Why don't you get it out? Get it all, why don't you? You wouldn't want the historians to miss out on anything. And after all, it's what you've been looking for all summer. It's maybe what you've been looking for for years. I'm going to enjoy seeing you hand it over to the historians, Pembroke. I'm going to enjoy it a lot."

"So that's why you came to Point Reyes," Pembroke said. "How did you know? Did your brother tell you? He wasn't much of a letter writer, but there was always the phone. I wondered—"

He broke off. Nick was staring at him in honest bewilderment. Pembroke took a deep breath, tried to smile. The cornered look was back in his eyes. Carefully, he got out a handkerchief, wrapped the little porcelain bowl in it, and put it back into his pocket, buttoning it for security.

Calling Richard a snoop. The vagueness—or not—of the bomb threat. The look in his eyes. Slowly, Nick stepped on board the wreck, ignoring the sudden shift it made to accommodate his weight. He had to be nearer to Pembroke. He had to be able to look into his face.

"So it *has* taken you years," Nick said, figuring it out as he went along. "Years of going through the archives, writing up the research, narrowing down places the frigate could be. I should have known. It must have taken a year at least to organize this field trip to cover your real reason to be here. And last summer Richard found out. He was your student, he had lots of reasons to be going through your papers. And he came across some research that had nothing to do with ecology. He would have been interested. He would have come to you about it. That's the way he was. He would never have believed he had anything to be afraid of. But he didn't believe in stealing, either. He wouldn't have liked the idea of you using Conservocean as

190

a cover for an illegal treasure hunt. He would have made the whole thing public. But he didn't have a chance to, did he? A bomb was placed on the ship on one of the few nights Richard slept on board, and he died."

"It wasn't like that," Pembroke said, his voice soft and rapid. "The bomb was set by mill workers. The Seattle police know it, they even know exactly who. They just can't prove it well enough to satisfy a judge, that's all. You go to them, you'll see. I didn't kill your brother. I warned him not to sleep on board. For God's sake, I told him!"

"Like you told Bill to fix his regulator? You told him and told him, you said. And he still didn't fix it. So that means he wasn't the kind to listen. Maybe Bill was the kind to deliberately not do something he was nagged about. Maybe you knew that about him. Nagging him, you could be sure he wouldn't listen, and you would have nothing to blame yourself for when he got into trouble because of it. And he did get into trouble, didn't he? He died. People die around you, Pembroke. You warn them, and they die."

Pembroke made a sudden violent movement forward, then checked himself. Neither of them noticed that his movement was echoed by one in the wreck. "Why in the name of God would I want Bill to die?"

"I suppose he would have had to get a share in the treasure."

"And naturally I knew that there was going to be an earthquake today, and that Bill would die without his tanks?"

"You didn't have to know it would be an earthquake. Diving, there are all kinds of dangerous situations. If it hadn't been an earthquake, it would've been something else."

"You're calling me a murderer," Pembroke said, a muscle jerking around his mouth. "I've never killed anybody or anything in my life."

"Maybe not. Maybe you just make it possible for somebody or something else to do your killing for you. That's the way it was with Richard, wasn't it? There was a bomb threat, and you made use of it. You told Richard not to sleep on board that night just to make sure he would. Because you knew Richard, you knew if you said there was danger, he'd go for it headfirst. That's what he was like. And when it was all over, you could just shrug your shoulders and say, Well, it isn't my fault he got bombed to bits. I warned him. *I'm* not a monster. It was all his own fault." Nick dashed at his eyes with a muddy hand. "But it *is* your fault he died. You manipulated him. You took advantage of what he was."

And in Nick's mind, mourning, was the thought: We should have done that, too. Instead, we warned him not to leave UBC, we told him he'd never get his degree with a man who played politics as much as Pembroke did. We warned him, and warned him, and it would have been better to have done the exact opposite. It would have been better to have used what he was against him, the way Pembroke did. At least, if we had, he would still be alive.

"It won't wash, kid," Pembroke said, cold and hard. "You're mad at your big brother for going away and leaving you, and it feels bad to be mad at a dead man, so you want to pin the blame on me. Even if I had known that Richard would stay on board that night just because I warned him, and I'm not for one minute admitting that I did, it was *Richard* who made the decision to stay, not me. And there might not have been a bomb. There was, but there might not have been. I didn't *know* it was going to happen. I haven't got one damn thing to feel guilty about, see?"

Nick stared at him. Pembroke believed what he was saying. He really believed it! "Because of you, Richard

192

slept on board that night, when he wouldn't have, otherwise. You haven't one damn thing to feel guilty about? You're just as much a monster as Drake, leaving all those men here to die!"

He leaped forward. What he intended to do to Pembroke, he didn't know, but he didn't have a chance to find out. His foot slipped on the mud that coated the wrecked hull, and he fell, sliding forward and slamming headfirst into the cannon. The wreck shifted alarmingly. Behind him he heard Pembroke shout something, but he couldn't make it out. Richard, he thought, lying face downward, retching, and crying a little. Oh, Richard.

And in his mind he seemed to hear a sound, deep, deep, like a foghorn moaning its warning tones, or something more human, grieving. *Water swirling and tides rising and the sea drowning the land and the land choking the sea. And so it goes on, and on, and he who is caught between the white water and the rocky shore, is it the water that kills him, or is it the land?*

Was it Pembroke who had killed Richard, or Richard who had killed himself with that bomb the mill workers had planted? And was Pembroke right when he said that Nick had blamed Richard for going away and leaving him? Blamed him for being vulnerable, when he had never seemed that way? Blamed him for not being permanent, for not being an adored older brother to be relied on forever? If Richard could not be permanent, nothing could be.

I did blame you, Richard.

Again, in his mind, the voice, deep and mournful. *The Song is deep, it sings all things. All things add to it, though not all harmonically.*

The wreck shifted again. Again Pembroke cried out. "That crevice is definitely getting bigger. For Christ's sake, get off the wreck!"

Another warning, Nick thought. Pembroke's specialty

was warning people he had good reason to want out of the way. You didn't heed those warnings, you died. Nick thought about it for a moment. It was just that much too long.

With a creak and a groan the old wreck began to move. Slowly at first and then not slowly at all, it slid down the widening crevice, and Nick slid with it, faster and faster. The sides of the crevice caved in as the wreck descended and mud poured in on Nick, covering him, burying him. He gasped for air, but there wasn't any to be found. He was drowning, drowning. His hand went out instinctively, rising above the mud, five fingers only, reaching for help, the rest of him gone. He touched metal—the cannon. Part of it was above the mud. His fingers closed around it, then hauled desperately. He was above the surface of the mud. Openmouthed, he gulped in great lungfuls of air, choking on the dirt in it, but grateful. His nostrils were no use; they were completely full of mud. He kept his mouth open, and then, when the gasping was less, he pried open his caked eyes.

Thinking fast, he grabbed the rope near where Pembroke had tied it to the cannon. He was alive, but he was at the bottom of the crevice. Pembroke was at the top, standing statue still on the solid rock ledge. He was holding on to the other end of the rope, still coiled, a lot of slack in between. His face staring down at Nick was full of hatred.

"You're not going to pull me up, are you?" Nick said hoarsely. "You're going to leave me here to die."

"I warned you to get off the wreck. I warned you twice!"

"I couldn't. I—"

Pembroke was still holding the other end of the rope. That was right, he wouldn't want to lose the rope, because it was tied to the cannon, and the cannon was mounted on the ship, and Pembroke still wanted its hold full of beloved Ming porcelain. Desperately, Nick tried to pull himself up by the rope, winding it around his waist first, but there was no resistance in the other end, and he only fell back, bringing down another torrent of mud on top of himself. Nick choked and gasped, then screamed at the top of his lungs. "Pembroke, this isn't like the others! If you do this, it's murder. Real murder this time, not just letting people die because they haven't done something they should have. Murder!"

He was screaming at nothing, only a snake of rope leading nowhere he could see. He was at the bottom of a crevice that was caving in all around him, and Pembroke was gone.

CHAPTER NINETEEN

WITH A SUCK AND A PLOP THE SPEAR came out of the mother whale's cheek. Marty fell backward into the mud. Blood spurted from the wound, then slowly stopped. Marty let go of the spear and dragged herself upright.

Are you all right? Does it hurt? Can I do anything?

You have done too much. Marty shrank back, dismayed by the whale's anger. The mother sighed slowly from her blowholes and looked at Marty with one huge, dark eye. *Unjust. It is not your fault but my own. You cannot help it that you are new, and that I cannot sing you into the past.*

Why should you want to? Marty asked, bewildered.

Because I thought the Song was repeating. I thought it was a refrain. And because I thought so, I began singing it so, making what happens now echo what happened then. And it was a mistake, little calf. You are the proof. You are here now, and you were not then, not in any guise, not even an echo. And yet you have significance. And so I was wrong, the Song was not written to be repeated. Yet I sang it so. And my singing made things happen that might not, had I not sung.

She went into herself then, and Marty went with her, absorbing into her own mind the mother's whalesong, her direct memories, her visions of the past, while still retaining all of what she herself was. With powerful double vision she saw a bay lined with tree-covered hills, smoke rising from roof holes in the distant native encampments, a camp near shore full of men in old-fashioned clothes;

196

and she knew that what she was seeing was the Estero a long time ago, when Drake had come here. She saw two sailing ships at anchor in the cove. One was rather short and narrow in the beam and carried two masts roped with tattered sails. It looked awkward and graceless and not very safe. The second ship was totally different: at least twice the size of the first, three masted and armed with many guns, higher at one end than the other, and with a look of speed and power to her. The *Golden Hind,* Marty thought. The first ship ever to sail all the way around the world and bring its captain home alive.

Drake was on the high stern of the *Hind* now, a short man, to appear so dominant. He had reddish brown hair and prominent, round, penetrating blue eyes. There were petulant lines around his mouth, hidden somewhat by his beard. He stood with his head held very high and his shoulders back, as if to gain stature, and his stocky body seemed all chest. A proud man, Marty thought, a man with a lot of things to prove. There was a boy with him, facing him down. She recognized him at once as the ragged, angry boy in her dream. Then he had reminded her of Nick, but this time she knew who he was: John Doughty, the boy who hated Drake so much and with such good reason.

A young man-singer and an older one, the mother whale sang, *and there was hatred between them, and things were done then that the People had to stop.*

And Marty saw those things, the beatings and the isolation and the time John had been thrown into the water, when the whales had come to his rescue. And she saw how when the careening of the *Golden Hind* was finished, Drake put John Doughty and twelve other men on board the frigate that could not sail out of sight of land, and told them he would come back and pick them up again someday. And she saw how he sailed then out of the Estero, while the natives lamented on the hilltops and the men on the frigate wept. And she saw when all but one of these men left the frigate and joined the natives on the hills; and not very long thereafter, when birds abandoned the Estero in masses of beating wings. And she heard in her own mind the echo of an ancient and terrible earthquake vibration screaming its warning to the whales, and saw them flee the Estero, all except two, who could not leave.

Another mother, and another calf, mourned the mother in Marty's mind. *The calf was injured and could not swim, and so the mother stayed. That mother watched the bigger log go away, and the smaller one remain behind. And she was there when the bay moved and the high places fell and the small log overturned and sticks within it broke and the young man-singer fell headfirst into the sea. He could not breathe, but though it was in Song already to help him, that mother could not leave her calf. Still, she was there, and watching, when the orca man-singer came back in his giant log, and took the young one out of the sea, and saved him.*

And Marty, listening, saw too; saw the *Golden Hind* return through whipping earthquake winds and tumbling rocks; saw Francis Drake stand on that tossing deck and throw a rope to the boy in the sea, the boy he hated because he reminded him of a killing that should not have been done, the boy who hated him because of a dead brother. And she saw how in the instant before the boy's fingers closed on the rope he almost refused it, and she saw how Drake almost let go of his own end when the other took hold. So much hate they had for each other, and yet the rope linked them. And neither, in the end, let go. Why had Drake come back for John Doughty? Why, when he had abandoned him already, had the earthquake made him return?

It is impossible to understand orcas, the mother whale said, *as impossible as it is to understand why the bay moves and the waters rush out of the shallows and leave the People*

198

stranded. It happened that day as it has happened now. That mother was stranded, as I have been stranded, and her calf's Song failed, as mine has failed. And she stayed and watched and put it to memory, and when the waters rushed in again, she let them lift her, up and up, and with all the strength of her flukes and her flippers she fought being dashed against the shore. And then, when the waters surged backward, she swam with them, for her calfling was gone and she had no reason now to stay. And so she rejoined her People and sang what she had seen, and so it came down to me. And now, in this time, another young man-singer and another older one have come to this same place with the same kind of hatred between them. And I thought it was a refrain, a part of the Song meant for repetition. I was the only singer here; I had a responsibility. And so I sang it, and forced the Song into repetition when it was not meant to repeat, and so the bay has swum again, and my own calfling's song is done.

Marty couldn't bear the grief in the mother's voice. From somewhere in the north, where distant People roamed and sang, she heard a thread of whalesong, and somehow she magnified it. Mind to mind she gave it to the mother, though she herself only dimly understood it. *Water swirling and tides rising and the sea drowning the land and the land choking the sea. And so it goes on, and on, and he who is caught between the white water and the rocky shore, is it the water that kills him, or is it the land? What does it matter? What is, is. There is no blame. You sang what was meant to be, or else you could not have sung it.*

There was a long pause. Marty stood still, leaning against the mother's vast side, two cold, muddy, grieving creatures, different yet the same. The mother breathed out, in, long and deep, accepting. *You have helped me, little calf. Help makes bonds, and bonds are always two-way. The waters will return here, as they returned that first time. They will roar into these shallows, a single moving high place of water curling white at the top and terrible. Even for one with the People's strength it will be perilous. You, little calf, and your tiny calfling over there, the two of you could not survive it. You must leave me now and seek the safety of the high places.*

But you're wounded. I can't just—

It is a small wound for one of the People. My song will not cease because of it. I will be lifted by the returning waters as that earlier mother was lifted, and I will swim as she swam, and I will rejoin my People, and the Song will go on.

I don't want to leave you.

Do you not?

Marty hung her head. Because more even than she wanted to stay with the mother, she wanted to go. She loved this whale, but she loved Kathy, too, and Junie, and Lynda and Sam, and she loved her mother and her father, though they were none of them her kind. And she loved Nick, oh, she loved Nick, and he *was* her kind, and she didn't know where he was or if he was even safe, and she wanted his arms around her and hers around him, she *needed* him, and she knew he needed her.

Deep and mournful, yet joyous, too, the mother sang. *The Song is deep, it sings all things. All things add to it, though not all harmonically. Edges surround us, white-water violent or gentle-calm and sweet. At every meeting place, soft-bodied creatures are stranded, shelled creatures are tossed up, mariners are wrecked, all because they have crossed over their own bounds. The wise know when to draw back. There are boundaries between us, little calf, but our songs meet. Whenever we listen we will hear each other, the soft harmony of two different singers looking at each other through clear water. Now take your tiny calfling with you, and go.*

Harmony, Marty thought. A seamless, perfect join. The one Song played for once and for all the way it had been written. She would remember the joy of it all her life.

And Marty kissed the cold, muddy cheek of the whale, where even now the wound was beginning to seal over, and she picked up the spear to lean on, and then she began, slowly and determinedly, to limp her way over to Kathy.

They hurried as fast as they could, but even so it seemed to take a long time to reach the place where once the cove and the shore had met. The bottom of the Estero was mostly deep mud or silt slippery with weed. Even without a bad ankle, the footing was treacherous. Again and again Marty thanked heaven that Kathy was with her. The little girl had been back and forth over the area so many times to get water for the whale, she had discovered how to find the harder ground amid all the soft. Ignoring the dead fish lying ball eyed and gaping all around them, she took Marty to shore that way, and though it was a winding, roundabout route, Marty was grateful. It saved her ankle for the climb up the cliff, a climb that might have to be made very quickly. There was a hot, strained feeling in the air, and when Marty looked over her shoulder, a band of silver glittered hard and still on the distant horizon, as if the sun were shining through a wall of water sitting there, motionless, gigantic.

Imagination, she told herself. A tsunami would surely not look like that, so bright and calm. But she hurried faster, so fast that it was Kathy who had to struggle to keep up, not her. They were on what was left of the beach, just past the place where the gate had thrown them to the ground, when movement on the cliff drew their attention.

"It's Dr. Pembroke," Kathy whispered. "What's he doing?"

Marty signaled her to be silent, and for once Kathy didn't argue. Pembroke had not seen them; would not, if they were careful, because their mud-covered bodies blended so well into their ruined surroundings. He was up on the path, at the place where it shouldered around the cliff, lying flat on his stomach and looking down at something below him in the dried-up pond. For the first time since the earthquake Marty remembered the wreck. She could see Pembroke in profile: the outthrust chin, the lines around the mouth, the rope end in his hand, the indecision. He didn't have a beard or blue eyes, so why did she think of Drake, and of John Doughty in the water, drowning?

What was down there, at the other end of that rope? Why was Pembroke holding it like that, so slack, as if it would take nothing at all to make him drop it?

"We have to climb up to where he is," she whispered in Kathy's ear. "But we can't let him see us too soon."

If he saw them too soon, from far away, he might think they hadn't noticed he was holding a rope. And then he might choose to drop it rather than allow them to see.

She thought of calling out something that would tell him she had seen the rope, but his hold on it was too loose. A sudden shout might shock him into dropping it by accident. And then whatever was on the other end of the rope could not be pulled up, and the tsunami would come and drown it forever.

She dropped to her hands and knees and began to crawl.

Nick had stopped shouting. Every time he did, more mud caved in on top of him. There was only Marty and Kathy to hear him, anyway, and what could they do against Pembroke, even if they could get here in time? It would only put them in danger, too. They wouldn't hear him, in any case. From the bottom of this narrow crack deep enough to devour a fleet of frigates, his voice carried about as far as if he were in a soundproofed room.

202

Except that this room had walls like wet cement, he thought, and those walls were slowly closing in on him.

There had been only tiny aftershocks since the earthquake. He would hardly have noticed them if it hadn't been for the way the mud kept dropping on him. A big aftershock was long overdue. When it came, the crack would slam shut, and the lost frigate with its precious Ming cargo would be gone. And Nick Young would be gone with it, no sign to show that he had ever been in the mud at all. By the time Pembroke got another chance to dig up the wreck, there probably wouldn't even be a body left to make him remember what he had done.

Hanging over the edge of the crack was the rope, very slack, twitching as Pembroke moved away. Nick had untied his own end from the cannon loop and fastened it firmly around his waist, but he had no hope at all that Pembroke would use it to pull him up. It made him hate the rope almost as violently and passionately as he hated the man who held the other end. Pembroke had as good as killed his brother, and now he was going to kill him, too. And no one would ever know. That was the worst of it. *No one would ever know.*

Nick closed his eyes and let hatred flow over him, thick and smothering. The impossibility of doing anything to relieve it was devastating. He opened his eyes, turning them upward to that narrow slit of blazing blue sky that was all he had left that wasn't mud. Even that was better than the darkness in his mind.

Alone. Since Richard had died, that was all Nick had wanted, to be left alone. Not to need anyone. He had thought he had it all figured out. Needing people meant you couldn't be safe because you were always at the mercy of the people you needed. Now Nick looked around and saw the truth, that being truly alone was terrible, that needing people was the only safety, as long as you needed the right ones.

Marty, I need you. I need your arms around me, I need mine around you, I need you.

He had needed Richard, too, and Richard had been the wrong person to need. Richard had had his own needs, and his own limits, his own boundaries that were nowhere near to Nick's. They had been like two unmatched shapes with a lot of space in between; they loved each other but could not really meet. Nick had thought Richard was abandoning him when he'd decided to join up with Pembroke, but that was wrong. Richard had never abandoned him, because he had never really been there for Nick that way at all.

He had blamed Richard for dying, too. He had thought Richard had brought his own death on himself by going away with Pembroke and getting involved in dangerous activities. And now he, Nick, had done the exact same thing. He had brought his own death upon himself by going down to Pembroke and talking to him and getting on the frigate with him and telling him the truth about himself, all very dangerous activities indeed. He had put his desire for revenge over his love for Marty. He had let her love for a whale, and his hatred for Pembroke, come between them.

Now, when he thought of her loving that whale, there was no resentment in him. If the whale and Marty had a meeting place that was even marginally close to being as perfect as his own and Marty's was, she would be infinitely the richer for it. And he wanted her richer, he wanted her happy, he wanted her to have all the love she needed and deserved, because he loved her. It was that simple.

It was only too bad that he had to be here, waiting to die, to find it out.

CHAPTER TWENTY

UNDER NORMAL CIRCUMSTANCES, MARTY and Kathy could never have gotten as close to Pembroke without him noticing them. But by the time they were halfway up the path where he would certainly have seen them, the circumstances were anything but normal. The first thing that happened was in the earth itself. It gave a slow, sickening roll, not a jolt, more like the initial languid drop in a roller-coaster ride, warning of things to come. Marty and Kathy were on their hands and knees, and Pembroke was lying flat, so none of them were rolled off the path, but they all instinctively clutched at the nearest solid-seeming object. For Marty it was the newly revealed root of one of the few bushes still remaining in the cliff wall. Kathy held on to Marty's right leg. And Pembroke, Marty saw with a relief that she couldn't explain, clutched the rope.

She didn't have long to be relieved. Out at sea, something blinked, a moving brightness with the sun glaring down on it. Big, wide, endlessly wide, high . . . She was caught by it, as Pembroke was caught, two horrified sets of eyes staring out at the approaching tsunami, while Kathy hid her head and sobbed. "Snakes," she cried, and the hissing it made did sound like that, snakes multiplying far out in Drake's Bay, two to four to forty to four hundred; thousands of snakes twining and hissing with louder and louder voices, so loud that Marty wouldn't have heard the muffled cry from down in the dried-up pond if she hadn't been waiting for it. But she did hear it, and knew whose it was: Nick, who was supposed to be in the camp with his computer; Nick, who was instead at the other end of Pembroke's rope. Which meant he couldn't get up by himself. Which meant he was at the mercy of a man he hated, and who now, Marty was sure, hated him.

Her heart leaped into her throat; she felt strangled, drowning already. Somehow, she got to her feet. Pembroke didn't see her; he was a man in a dream, staring first at the approaching wall of water, then down to the rope in his hand, then farther down to Nick, then at the water again.

"Pull him up!" Marty shrieked. He didn't seem to hear. She hauled Kathy to her feet. "Up. Up to the bluffs. As fast as you can, and don't stop once you get there."

"But I'll have to climb right over—" She pointed to Pembroke, still lying there as if dazed.

"I said *go!*"

Kathy was gone. Marty limped after her. Slow, so slow. Kathy was already just about up to where Pembroke was, whereas she—

Pembroke still hadn't moved anything but his gaze. Out toward the tsunami, then down at the rope, then farther down, then out toward the tsunami again. Over and over, shock or indecision or both, and Nick at the bottom of that slack and useless rope, Nick! Marty screamed again and again, but the noise was lost in the hiss from the bay, and she doubted if Pembroke would have heard, anyway. When Kathy leaped over him, she might have been a ghost for all he noticed.

I'll have to take the rope from him, she told herself.

But that meant she would have to get there. Faster. Forget your ankle. Faster. There was no pain. She would not allow there to be any pain. Near now, so near. She would take the rope from Pembroke, and somehow, somehow she would pull Nick up.

Smash! Marty almost fell. The tsunami had hit the coast, not here, but farther up. Only a minute or two before it would be the Estero it was slamming into. *Smash! Smash!* Marty scrambled on. She was at Pembroke's side, bending for the rope. It might have been that he saw her and knew she would be a witness to his refusal to help Nick, though he didn't look at her or acknowledge her presence in any way. It might simply have been that the smashing of that enormous wall of water against the cliffs of Chimney Rock galvanized him, releasing him from shock. Or it might have been, as Marty believed to her depths, that he had come to the same inexplicable decision that Francis Drake had, when he had turned the *Golden Hind* around and gone back to save his enemy.

The wise know when to draw back.

For whatever reason, Pembroke was suddenly on his feet, and the rope was taut in his hand. "All right, come up!" he said, his face turned into a mask, and though it wasn't loud, Marty heard it through all the smashing and breaking stone, through all the hissing and roaring and splashing. And then he was pulling, pulling with all his might, hauling in on the rope, hand over hand, until its clean, white length grew black and heavy, until a mud-covered boy came up over the edge and Nick was there.

Nick said nothing to Pembroke. He didn't even look at him. In his blackened face his eyes looked amazingly blue. He looked only at Marty.

"She needs an arm up," Pembroke said roughly. "Look at her ankle. Here, I'll take one side and you—"

"Thanks," Nick said. For a moment only they looked at each other, enemies to the end, and then they each put a shoulder under one of Marty's arms, and hand to hand, linked, they ran her up the path.

The tsunami poured Niagara-like over the sandbar, then on into the Estero itself. Nick, holding onto Pembroke's hand behind Marty's back, was too deafened by the roar to hear his own shout. They were near the top of the path, but the giant wave would arrive before they could get there. Nick pushed Marty and Pembroke against the cliff face, found a tough root to hang on to, closed Marty's hands on it, closed his on hers, and looked over his shoulder. He had to see it. He had to know whether he was going to die or not.

It was an appalling spectacle. The central part of the wave had found the sandbar no obstacle, but the bluffs on either side of the Estero were a barricade the water couldn't breach. The force of the impact was like nothing Nick had ever heard: a bowling alley gone mad, a million bolts of cloth ripping to shreds. He wanted to clap his hands over his ears but didn't dare loosen his grip on Marty's hands. He saw her face wide eyed with horror. He couldn't reassure her. Spray streamed down on them like rain.

The tsunami, its width reduced by the bluffs but still formidable, surged into the mud plain that had been the Estero. Hanging on for their lives, the three people on the path felt the reverberation as the gigantic wave struck the outer wall of their own cliff. The cliff broke. The entire corner, top to bottom, fell in a single, clean-edged piece. Water roared backward, thrusting into the peaceful cove, deluging the sand dunes and the memorial to Sir Francis Drake, drowning the frigate that he had left here all those centuries before.

It would have drowned him, too, Nick knew, if Pembroke hadn't pulled him up. He didn't like the thought. It meant he had to be grateful to Pembroke, and he didn't want to be. Pembroke had tried to kill him. He held on to that thought, watching the wave flow inland.

"The water didn't go as high as I thought it might," Pembroke said now, and Nick was surprised to find he could hear him. The tumult had lessened, water pouring inland smoothly and silently, turning what had been four separate bays into one. "It'll surge out again, it has to. After that it'll be like an accordion, forward and back, forward and back, until all the force of it is spent. But we're safe enough. If that first one didn't reach us . . . Got to hand it to Drake. He knew how to pick his anchorages." He shook his head, smiling ruefully.

Nick stared at him silently. So Pembroke thought he was in the clear. He had saved Nick's life; nobody could say he hadn't. He'd helped save Marty's as well. There was no longer any dead whale or spear out in the Estero to cause people to ask awkward questions. If the wreck had gone, as well as the guideline to it (Nick having untied the rope from the cannon to put around his waist instead), nevertheless Pembroke had a pretty good idea where it was and could come back to it anytime he could think up a good reason for being there. Yes, it was all very nice for Dr. Raymond Pembroke. All except for one thing.

Nick watched Pembroke's eyes, deliberately not looking at the little bulge in the other man's pocket in case Pembroke should remember it. A single tiny piece of Ming dynasty porcelain: It was a small thing, to ruin a man. But it would be enough.

You made my brother kill himself, Nick said silently to those confident hazel eyes. You would have killed me. You're a thief and a liar and a phony and I'm going to tell the world what you are. I'm going to tell them what really happened to Richard, and why. I'm going to tell them how your Conservocean field trip here this summer was just a cover to help you steal treasure. And I'm going to prove it with that bowl in your pocket, Dr. Pembroke. I'm going to ruin you.

Help makes bonds, said a deep, cool darkness in his mind.

No, Nick thought. He helped me, but only because he

had to. Marty would have told people if he hadn't. There's no bond between us.

Nick's left arm, under Marty's right shoulder, Pembroke's right under Marty's left. Two hands gripping each other behind her back, an unacknowledged bridge carrying Marty to safety.

I told him what he was, I made him admit it to himself, I pushed him to the brink, and he didn't go over. For whatever reason, he didn't go over.

Bonds are always two-way.

The hand on the rope, pulling to safety; the hand on the other end, allowing itself to be pulled. Who saved whom, in that moment? Whose was the victory?

And Nick remembered John Doughty, who could not forgive Drake and wanted revenge, who took him to court and tried to ruin him and who was, in the end, ruined himself.

Ruin, too, was a two-way street.

Nick dropped his eyes, let them rest meaningfully on Pembroke's bulging pocket, looked up again, and saw that the man had remembered. "I'm—going back to camp," Pembroke said, his voice unusually hesitant. "I should find out if everything's all right."

He waited, as if asking permission. Nick said nothing. After a moment, Pembroke went away.

Marty was staring and staring into waters that heaved and boiled in the Estero. Nick knew she was looking for flukes or a spout, or maybe a great baleened head thrusting itself through the water. "The whale will be all right," he said softly.

"She said she would be," Marty said.

Nick took her hand between both his own, holding it very tight. "I think you should believe her," he said.

They were silent then for a long time. Nick was thinking about Vancouver, and his father, and the graveyard he had never let himself see. "I'll be going home at the end of the week," he said at last.

She nodded, but said nothing, only waited.

"I expect you will be, too. Somehow I can't imagine the field trip going on with all this wreckage around."

Still nothing.

"You live in Vancouver, too. What do you do there?"

"Besides baby-sit? I go to school. I was thinking of quitting this fall, but now . . ." She smiled a little. *You have significance,* the mother whale had said to her. "Well, now I think I'm going to wait and see."

"You'll see *me,* won't you?" It came out in a rush.

She looked into his eyes, and he knew the answer. His arms went around her body, and hers around his. Two bodies, one edge between them one meeting place—perfect, if a little muddy.

Kathy came down from the hill. "Marty. Hey, Marty! Did ya see me run? I bet even Junie couldn'ta gone that fast."

Nobody answered her. She put on a brave smile. "I'm still bleeding, though. Want to see?"

Nobody did.

"Pigs," she said loudly, and, "I'm going to look for Junie."

"We all will," Marty said.

They walked side by side, Kathy in the middle. Now and then, when they saw the damage the earthquake had brought to their beautiful Point Reyes, they would become very quiet. But that was what Point Reyes was and what it had always been: a land under siege, moved about by earthquakes, battered by storms, obscured by fog, eroded by the sea. It wasn't still and it wasn't constant. Its edges were always new and its boundaries always changing. It was what made it magical.

Today they were part of that magic. They knew that Sam and Lyn and Junie would be safe, they knew that the

211

camp would be a wreck but that it wouldn't matter, they knew that all the people they cared about would show up, and that was all that counted right now. They had made it through another vast rubbing together of continental edges, and they were safe.

Out in the gulf of the Farallons, a single gray whale swam slowly and steadily into the north. She sang as she swam, a deep and melancholy lament that had yet some hope in it. After a long time she fed, and it was good to feel the hard-backed creatures between tongue and baleen while the waters grew colder and yet more cold. A long time after that she heard singing, very far away but recognizable. The People, she thought. Her People. And when she sang out her answer to them, her Song was not melancholy, and the hope was stronger.

Renewal, she sang, *always, after an end, there is renewal.*